The lonely
margins
of the sea

SHONAGH KOEA is a fulltime writer who lives and works in Auckland. She has published four novels including *The Wedding at Bueno-Vista* (1996) and two collections of short stories. Her short fiction has appeared in magazines, mainly the *Listener*, since 1981 when she won the Air New Zealand Short Story Award. She has received many awards since, including the Queen Elizabeth II Literature Committee Writing Bursary (1989 and 1992), the Fellowship in Literature (1993) at the University of Auckland, and the Buddle Findlay–Sargeson Fellowship in Literature (1997). Her novel *Sing To Me, Dreamer* was shortlisted for the Arts Council of New Zealand Book Awards for Fiction in 1995, and was read on National Radio the following year. Shonagh Koea has given lectures and readings at the International Festival of the Arts in Wellington, the Canberra Word Festival, the *Listener* Women's Book Festival, and for the New Zealand Book Council.

The lonely
margins
of the sea

SHONAGH KOEA

V

VINTAGE

*The author wishes to thank
the Sargeson Trust
for awarding her the Buddle Findlay-Sargeson Fellowship
from 1 February 1997 to 31 May 1997
which enabled her to write a large part of this novel.*

Vintage New Zealand
(An imprint of the Random House Group)

18 Poland Road
Glenfield
Auckland 10
NEW ZEALAND

Sydney   New York   Toronto
London   Auckland   Johannesburg
and agencies throughout the world

First published 1998

© Shonagh Koea 1998
The moral rights of the Author have been asserted.

Printed in Malaysia
ISBN 1 86941 348 2

To the memory of Small, my most beloved white Manx cat
who died on 10 October 1997 as I was finishing this novel.
She always sat on my desk as I wrote.
Au revoir, my dearest friend.

One

THE WOMAN CALLED Stephanie drove south late in the morning, telling deliberate but innocent lies before she left the city and, again, when she finally arrived in the evening as the moon rose yellow in a bright, bold sky. The doorbell rang urgently through the old house, up the stairs, out into the back wing where they always kept the garden chairs folded during winter. Her cold hand urgent upon the button, from far away she heard the sound of slow footsteps approaching. Her cousin Louise must have been in the kitchen, she thought and, standing on the step, considered the sudden idea that it must be impossible to obliterate the architectural maps of the mind, the memory of sounds and their origins — and, the recollection of scents. The distinctive essences of mothballs, camphor chests, dried flowers, old carpets and ancient but delicious toilet soap of brands long obsolete greeted her as the door swung open, infinitely forgotten till that moment, then swiftly and infinitely remembered.

'Did you have a good journey?' said Louise. There was no other greeting, no hello, no exclamation of delight. And this was not caused by apathy or neglect. Stephanie stood for a moment, the weight of the small suitcase suddenly almost unbearable. It was long familiarity that caused the reticence, deep-seated and profoundly understood affection, almost like an illness. They had the same blood, the same bones, the same colouring, so greetings might be superfluous, almost as if they said hello to themselves in a mirror, even after all this time and after everything that had happened.

'Yes, it was a good trip.' That was the lie. 'I thought you'd be in bed,' she said. 'And no, you can't carry my bag.' Louise had stretched out a willing arm, the other one folded against her chest like a wounded wing. 'You can't do that. I expected —' And here she stopped. It would have been difficult to say what she had expected. Certainly not a brightly lit house and the smell of dinner cooking, Louise pale but neatly dressed and wearing a gingham apron. 'I thought you'd be in bed,' she said again, and left it at that.

'Which room am I in? I'll just run upstairs and throw my bag in the door then,' and she went swiftly up the old staircase that, like the scent of the house, was infinitely forgotten and now suddenly and most terribly remembered, over the first landing where the stairs turned towards the front gables and where, years ago, there was always a dolls' pram made of seagrass and full of old French dolls in lace dresses.

Where's Stephanie? Stephanie's been a naughty girl again. Steph-anie's gone up the stairs. Stephanie's at those dolls again. And there would be her mother climbing the stairs behind her as she stood, finally triumphant, with a small hand on one of the toys at last. You're a naughty, naughty girl. The hand would take hers in a grip that crunched her knuckles together. You know you've been told not to come up here. You're not allowed up here, you know that. You've been told to stay in the kitchen. How many times do I have to say it? And down the stairs they would go, twin shadows grotesque in some distant twilight, roped together by the insubstantial bruise of their shadowy hands bitterly linked on the old wall.

Now she made no shadow at all, filtering down the unlit stairs to the back wing of the house, to the kitchen where Louise waited, the way known by heart from childhood and never forgotten, her small suitcase just a dark splurge like blood left behind on the carpet inside the upstairs bedroom door.

'What happened to the dolls' pram?' she asked later as Louise took roast beef from a foil dish. 'And do you want me to carve that meat?'

'No.' Louise's voice was too swift, she thought, too loud. 'It's been done already. The neighbours brought it in a while ago for our dinner, ready for when you arrived in the cold. They thought they should cook dinner for us. They've carved it already. They said we shouldn't have to worry about things like that, not tonight.'

She had not arrived till dusk and Louise was allowed to leave the hospital at two in the afternoon. The intervening hours in the house could have been long, solitary and even frightening. The neighbours must have rustled about, perhaps wondering if someone would even arrive at all. Tales of a distant cousin arriving at an unspecified time from the north — well, such tales have a flimsy air about them, even as a throwaway remark over a back fence in bright sunlight. My cousin has been allowed to come and look after me. Was it true? Could it be believed? And what cousin exactly? Surely not that cousin? And there could have been an emphasis on the word 'that', perhaps a raising of the eyebrows. Surely not her — not that one who once lived down the road in the old house behind all the trees, the place where you could see only the chimneys till a couple bought it and improved it no end. The first thing they did was clear the section, and then the hedges went under a bulldozer, and a good thing too. And they applied for a new number in the street after the trial because they didn't want to be known as the people who lived where she had lived. If I had my way, I'd bring back the birch and the hangman's noose. An eye for an eye, a life for a life. Might they have thought and talked like that? They called themselves 17A in the street now. Number 19 had been expunged. Louise had said so in one of her letters, even though the section was a full one, not a half site, and ranged over more than three-quarters of an acre of what the real estate agents had once called light woodland.

There was a long silence in the kitchen. 'The dolls were sold,' said Louise, 'a long time ago. The dolls would have been sold — I don't know how long ago. Seven years ago? Eight? I've forgotten.'

'They were French. They were valuable. I hope you got a good price.' Stephanie looked discreetly sideways, to where the old stove used to be, before the redecorations and the rebuilding. In her absence, the kitchen must have been refitted. Perhaps Louise had mentioned it in her letters, but the information might have been overlaid by her own more pressing problems at the time. The trial. The transfers over the years to other establishments where the fences were lower, the barbed wire less vicious but the rooms were still locked at night and all the windows were small. Louise's cupboards were all new now, with walnut doors. The old kitchen table with its red Formica top had gone. They were sitting at a new round mahogany one with matching chairs, and the curtains were yellow linen, not the old red gingham. Over where the new kitchen bench had been placed beneath an additional easterly window there used to be a dresser where carving knives and the steels upon which they were sharpened were kept in a felt-lined drawer, but there was nothing there now except the glittering new sink with taps so convoluted they looked theatrical and a granite bench with a cupboard beneath that must hold dishwashing detergent and the dishcloth. The knives, the cutlery, must be kept somewhere else now.

'How many potatoes?' Louise still had that one arm folded against her chest, wielding the spoon with the other hand, the dexterity miraculous.

'Just one.' She sat regarding this vegetable on her plate, pale and cheerless as an enemy's eye, and wondered if Louise's failure to answer meant that the price for the dolls had been distressingly low and was now regretted, or was so high it could not be divulged. They had always been a secretive family. They confided in no one, not even themselves.

'It was good of you to come.' Louise sat down and began to eat as if she were taking afternoon tea with a visiting vicar. 'I hope you don't mind having dinner in the kitchen.'

'I always used to have dinner in the kitchen,' she said, 'when I was a little girl, years ago, when I tried to play with the dolls on the landing. It was my greatest ambition.'

'Wouldn't they let you?'

'No.'

'I wonder why,' said Louise. 'I wouldn't have minded at all. I don't think I ever played with them myself. And I'd have been grown up by then and wouldn't have given a damn about the dolls. Salt? Pepper? I hope the meat's all right? It is? Good — and I hope you don't mind it being carved already. They' — and she nodded vaguely towards a window that looked on to the next door house — 'were just trying to help, to make sure we had nothing to do.' The explanation seemed too plausible, too logical, too nice.

'Yes, indeed.' Once she had been asked why she often said yes indeed, just like that, anonymous and pleasant but slightly uninterested, and she had told the questioners that it was her own way of cutting herself off from people, from a person, with a mindless and meaningless pleasantry. And, while she watched, the man in the middle of the row, the one brought in especially to question her, had written several swiftly shaped sentences on a pad he had placed on the table in front of him. Secretive. Devious. Those might have been two words he used. You never knew what they thought or wrote. Perhaps he had divined she was afraid. Frightened. Perhaps he had written that kinder and more accurate summing up of her thoughts then.

There is still the discrepancy of an hour and a half not accounted for, he had said. We have still not completely explored the difference in time. Could we go through it all again, please? Or perhaps you might like to have a rest? We could talk to you later? They took it all slowly, pussyfooting through the questions.

'Why didn't you ever play with the dolls yourself?' She was picking up the cutlery now, an innocent fork with flat tines and a knife with a wide blade. Louise must have bought new cutlery, Scandinavian and expensive, blunt and innocuous, to go with the new kitchen.

'I couldn't be bothered. I didn't like dolls much. I don't think anyone ever played with them.'

'Well,' said Stephanie and listened to her own voice become slow with recollection, 'I would have liked to, but I suppose it doesn't really matter now, does it — not this long time later?' But the memory of being allowed to play only in the kitchen and not with the dolls remained within the framework of a life like a label. A kitchen child with no dolls. So that was another lie she had innocently told, out of politeness, about things not mattering when they did, before she went up to bed in the big front room under the eaves, finally lying on the old kapok mattress with the stillness of extreme exhaustion so that, the following morning, the mark of her body lay like that of a corpse fallen into concrete.

'Goodnight, Stephanie.' Louise had kissed her cheek out on the landing before turning and going into her own bedroom. 'Thank you for coming,' she repeated. 'I must say you're looking well. A bit pale, but well. And you don't look a day over thirty-two. I didn't think you'd be so pale but it's understandable — I suppose you'd get out of the habit of going outside, wouldn't you. We aren't very fond of the sun, anyway. It's the fair skin, my mother always used to say. The sun doesn't agree with us. Anyway, goodnight. Sleep well. I'll see you in the morning.'

'Yes, indeed.' As Stephanie watched, Louise's bedroom door closed and there was the sound of the key turning in the lock.

'Stephanie, I forgot to say' — the voice sounded muffled by the stout door and the big copper lock — 'that since the burglaries I always lock my bedroom door. There's a key in your door — you can lock yours if you like. I usually do. Please don't be offended.' There was the sound of retreating footsteps.

Louise slept at the back of the house, looking out over where the old vegetable garden used to be, in a room she had had since she was seven years old. In her brief glimpse before the door closed, Stephanie had seen that there was still a teddybear on a chest beside Louise's oak hoop-back bed, which was in the same position it had always occupied, backed into an embrasure in a wall that had been formed by the downstairs chimney soaring up through the height of the house.

'Goodnight,' she called through the locked door. 'Everything's going to be fine, you'll see. There's nothing to worry about.' More lies. 'If you hear me moving around for a while, don't be alarmed. I often sit and write for a while before I go to sleep. I can use the dressing table as a desk. I can manage perfectly.' She waited for a moment. 'Are you quite sure you really want me to be in the front room — the best room?' The front bedroom had always been the best, always occupied by other people, by well-upholstered aunts and cousins who had velour coats with fox fur collars, nightdresses hand-embroidered by nuns in distant convents, red velvet dressing gowns with quilted revers. Never herself.

'Oh, um —' The muffled voice seemed to be drawing closer and there was a rattle of the key in the lock again. A sliver of a view of Louise appeared briefly as the door opened a crack. 'That's okay,' she said. 'It's really the only one that's ever used these days, except for mine. It's not really the best room any more. It's kind of just the room, the only room for anyone. Sleep well.' The door closed again.

'I will.' That was another lie. The lies told before the journey were simpler.

Yes, of course I remember the way. I must have driven over that road dozens and dozens of times. I know it — knew it — like the back of my hand. Forgotten how to drive a car? Isn't it like riding a bicycle and you never forget? Or fornicating, she had wanted to say, but did not. She slid behind the wheel of her car and sat there with an air of calm. Another lie, but one of mode, of behaviour. But where is first gear, she had thought and then saw the diagram on the knob of the gear lever, slowly pressing the clutch with a tentative foot. You see, she had said, it's easy really. You never forget. Off you go then, Stephanie. Someone had slapped the roof of the car. Cheerio. Oh, by the way, Stephanie, your car — you're probably wondering about your car. It's been up on blocks. Someone stored it for you all this time. He says it's all been checked and there's a new battery so you should be okay. Stop at any garage after you've been on the road about two or three hours and get some petrol. Think of it as a psychological exercise, Stephanie. Buy some petrol, talk about the weather, ask for directions even if you don't need them. There's a bit of cash in the glovebox, enough to get you through. Do the old marks out of ten thing, just as a project, like I've taught you. Good luck. Another slap on the roof. She had eased the car into first gear and felt it begin to move. There, she had said out the window, it's easy. Please don't worry.

But that conversation had been a flimsy architecture of small, gentle, saving fabrications. The traffic was all changed now. The roads had been altered. The signs were differently coded, but still she had pressed res-olutely south, sliding through the countryside like a secret. Four out of ten for inner doubts. Nine out of ten for fudging up the nerve to put on a mask of outward and false calm.

'Don't you stock honeycomb chocolate?' she had asked the man behind the counter at the service station when she stopped, nearly three hours away from the city.

'Honeycomb chocolate?' he said. 'That hasn't been around for years. Where've you been?'

'Oh, never mind then,' she had said, 'it was just a thought.' And she had climbed back in the car as if the request might have been just an ordinary error made out of absent-mindedness.

Two

THE HIGHWAY SOUTH is better signposted now but the café called Cowboys still sits enticingly and sweetly under its chocolate-coloured paint beside the main road at Ohinewai. A mile or two further on, the old cottage that used to sag on the road's edge has been renovated now and has roses over the front verandah.

She had driven quietly past all these faintly remembered sights that day, alone in the car and without any noise except the drum of tyres on the road or the muted sounds of distant traffic. The car had never had a radio, and it never would now because it was too old. And so was she, she thought as she slowed down, watching for the painted arrow to the right that would show her the quick way southward. She was too old, and too tired for such a journey, too tired for everything. And, at that moment, saw the arrow, like a dart straight into her recollection of other long ago journeys on that road when her expectation of the destination had been different and before she finally decided never to go back there again.

At the turn-off she sought, by the service station, the road was much wider than she remembered and no one could get lost there now because the signs were better and brighter than they used to be, the route more clearly marked. Years ago, she had habitually become lost at that point, nosing the car this way and that among the little streets, trying to find the bypass into the golden hills to the west. The car, now, seemed to know that way, to remember the last time she had gone over this road. Then she had been travelling north, the mirror image of the trip she took now, and the car was newer, its paint less dulled by the years, before it had been up on blocks for so long. Before her expression ceased to retain any look of absorption, concentration or expectation and long before the man at the dinner party said, 'You really annoy me, Stephanie. That is your name, isn't it? Stephanie? I don't like you. You've got a nerve, I must give you that. You've certainly got a nerve. People like you cost the ordinary taxpayer millions and then you come to a dinner party as if nothing's happened. I don't admire people like you, Stephanie. If I had my way I'd lock you up and I'd throw away the key,' and had turned away to the woman on his other side, the bright one who looked at him as if he were interesting and who said, 'You must tell me the story of your life, Martin.'

And while she had listened, he did begin to tell the other woman about his life. And no one at the dinner party had noticed, in the midst of the candlesticks and chatter and the other women who were all with partners and wore bright, large jewels on small, pale fingers, that she had begun to cry with her face turned away from his contemptuous tailored shoulder.

A stranger, the man with the notebook said. Why should you care what a stranger thinks? I don't. It was just embarrassing, that's all. I felt embarrassed. I hadn't realised things like that might happen, he said. People volunteer for these things, you know. They're very carefully vetted. It doesn't matter, she had said. The people who gave the dinner were very nice. It wasn't their fault. He was just a rude man, a bastard. They didn't know what he'd said. Would you like to go again, Stephanie? It's a pre-parole sort of thing, to help you get used to things. I am used to things, thank you. I think I'm fine in my own way, except for rude people. Rude people are a thing I've never been good at.

The car, on that other journey she had believed was final, had been mounded up with her favourite things, the ones she refused to let the removal men handle, and she had travelled slowly northward, taking the bends with care, getting lost on the way, burdened down with the accoutrements of a life she had been trying to salvage but which had been irrevocably lost later in the time it would take a butcher to slice a piece of topside in half. Just one arm movement, and a few seconds, and the life was gone.

Driving southward now she tried to remember what she had had in the car with her that other time, and failed. It might as well have all been left behind, she thought, as she easily found the road to the hills. It should have been sold with all the rest of the stuff when the old house back home, with the garden the agents had called woodland, was auctioned.

Halfway down the bypass, when she had been held by the hills for about half an hour, the mist rolled in from the sea and a stinging rain came down so she could see very little, and was glad because it was possible to travel without recollection. Earlier she had passed privet hedges blazing with small blooms. Sometimes ancient and forgotten pear trees, islanded by the ragged fences of derelict farm cottages, dragged larger and sweeter flowers across paddocks rich with buttercups. The countryside had spread out before her, the rolling high country trapping her with width and warmth, and when she was finally enclosed by the treacherous arms of that land she found herself suddenly caged again by the mist from the lonely margins of the sea.

It was like the distant evening when the policeman in his plain clothes, so that he looked like any man you might see anywhere, fetched her a cup of coffee and a sandwich and got a doctor to come from somewhere in that faceless building to listen to her chest because she was having trouble breathing. What seemed like the exercise of pleasantries was actually a gilded trap, but there was no need for that. She would have told them anyway because concealment was not something she had ever considered and she had gone there specifically to tell them, taking the knife with her so she could give it to them, stained from her own red hands.

'I don't see what the fuss is about,' she had said then. 'I've told you. As far as I'm concerned there isn't a problem. I'm guilty.' And when they gave her those long, searching looks, she said, 'I'm guilty, I am,' as if that would, somehow, make it better.

Defendant seemed flippant at the time, said a sergeant at the trial, and seemed to make jokes about the situation. It was difficult to see where she was coming from during the interrogation. She said several times, I don't see what the fuss is about.

Three

THE MAN AT the service station may have intended to say something else. He might not have been going to say, 'Aren't you Stephanie Beaumont? Don't I recognise you? Haven't I seen your picture in the paper?' He might have intended to say, 'Aren't you going to let me check the oil and water for you, lady? It's blowing up rough and you're travelling south right into it.' Or he might have said, 'Aren't you going to have a look at our really wonderful gift store before you head south? The wife stocks a lot of good lines that people often find very useful with the festive season coming up, not just the normal peanuts and lollies. She gets a lot wholesale from the East — hand-painted candles and that type of thing.'

He might have intended to make any remark of that sort, not necessarily what I imagined, not what had frightened me. And I may have got his contempt about the honeycomb chocolate out of proportion. Take a mark off. Honeycomb chocolate must be a superseded line now, but it is innocent enough, nevertheless. It could have been anything like that, not actual recognition, which sent me skidding out on to the highway again and away far to the south where the sea awaited.

They taught me to give myself marks out of ten, to analyse and assess my own behaviour and to mark myself accordingly. So I have given myself seven. I have taken two marks off because I did not wait to find out what the man meant before becoming alarmed and that is a negative action against myself. I have deleted another single mark for general morbidity because I cried when I saw the sea. There was no need for this because the sea has been there for a long time and I knew it was there.

I knew I would see the sea as I breasted that last hill before the coast, so there was no need to cry. Criss-cross with the mythical black pen. Two marks off. One mark off. And another mark off for the chocolate. Do better next time. Take yet another mark off the total for being too hard on yourself. There is no need for self-flagellation. Everyone makes mistakes, Stephanie, and small ones are not of great importance. Do you think you're possibly too hard on yourself? That is what they used to say to me, and I remember it now as I scribble my way through the night in the old front bedroom. Five out of ten.

I call them they because they altered over the years. One man with a notebook became another. I'm being moved on through the system, Stephanie. I won't be here next month. You'll find another doctor here when you have your appointment in March, but he'll have all your details and I'm sure you'll find he's very nice. Sometimes it was she. It'll be just the same as me, Stephanie, have no fear. Just a different face. You learn not to get attached to things, to people. So I called them all they. They said. They did. They told me. They recommended. No names. Nothing. Just they. Perhaps, similarly, they called me she, or Room 46, or appointment number three every second Wednesday, the quiet one who's no bother, just studies the leaves and doesn't want to go anywhere any more, that one. Reddish blonde hair, thin face, eyes that can look grey or green. The reader, the one who writes in her room till the lights go out sharp at nine.

Stephanie, most people recover from these things, do believe me. That's what they used to say. One of my people from here — I never use the word patient — now lives down near Wellington. He's got a very nice little business and he's managed to find a partner, from a dating agency I gather. They cater for all age groups, so I believe. They had a child last Christmas and he seems to have put it all behind him. You pay the price, Stephanie, and then you move on. He actually killed three strangers in cold blood on a drug trip but with proper therapy and the correct medication, Stephanie, he's fine now. We see his partner regularly and she makes sure he takes the pills and I don't see any further problem there. I've never believed for a moment that there's any problem with you, Stephanie. It was a one-off thing. If your depression at that time had been correctly diagnosed and treated, the incident would never have happened. You have never manifested any psychotic symptoms,

Stephanie. Believe me — I'd know. If you were a murderer born and bred I'd know, believe me. But I am a murderer. No, Stephanie, take a mark off for being too severe. You are merely a person who killed someone. Is there a difference? Yes, in my terminology, there is. If you had been in France, Stephanie, you would have got off. It would have been called a *crime passionnel*, and you would have got off. People would have sent flowers. You would have been on television when you were released after the trial, if there even were a trial, which I doubt. It's a shame the incident didn't occur in France, Stephanie, and I'm not entirely joking when I say that. Pick your country better next time.

So here we are — the incident. I should tell you about the incident, what the incident involved. It is late, though, and the incident does not ornament midnight very well. The incident, at midnight, may seem truly terrifying. Another day, perhaps. Another night.

Tell me some of your thoughts, Stephanie. I've got some extra time today. I can spend a bit more time here than usual. Tell me, what have you been reading? I always look forward to hearing about what you've read. It gives me hints about what to look for in the library myself. You're a wonderful reader. They used to talk to me nicely, really, as if I might have been visiting their house. As if I might have been an ordinary guest.

I'm reading this novel about a family. It's about an aunt, really, and a niece and they never liked each other till they didn't have anyone else left in the world and then they became quite close. Then the aunt loved the niece and the niece was very kind to the aunt. It's a really good book. You'd enjoy it, I feel sure. I used to chatter away to them like that.

I never said that I often thought about the sea. The sea had nothing whatever to do with me or their questions or the reasons why the questions were posed. If I had to say why I came to love the idea of the sea so much, it was because I decided the sea was always new. The tide comes in, the tide goes out. It takes away the dross and the dirt. Then the sea returns a few hours later and cleans the shore all over again. I would like to lie down on the sand and let the sea wash over me and make me clean and new again.

But if I had told him that, the kindly and questioning doctor who liked reading, then he would have said, so Stephanie, you feel dirty, do you? You feel in need of cleansing, do you? And he would have begun to write in his notebook. So I always just said I was fine. How are you,

Stephanie? Fine. Any bad dreams lately, Stephanie? No, I'm fine, thank you. Someone in your block has reported that they often hear you calling out in your sleep. Me? You must be joking. If I did call out, I'd just be singing. Singing, Stephanie? At two in the morning? Yup, you can sing anytime. I sing anytime. Don't take any notice of those tale-telling old slags — I don't even speak to them. Is there anything you often think about, Stephanie? I'm asking you that because it doesn't seem much use asking you about your dreams. Okay then — sometimes I think about the shops. By shops I mean just shops in a general sense. I was always very fond of looking at the shops. I used to shop a lot when my husband was alive, before all this, but I had the money then and I never thought about it. I suppose you could say I was once an I-shop-therefore-I-am sort of person. That used to be a bumper sticker but I suppose it isn't any more. I do miss going shopping but, I mean, there are lots of things to look at here. I study the colour of the rocks and the colour of the stones and sometimes, when I go out for my walk, I study yellow leaves and other times I might look specifically at just green shiny leaves. There's plenty to look at here so the idea about the shops — well, it doesn't really worry me, not any more. Stephanie, do please bear in mind that you've been transferred here because we firmly believe you're a very low risk. There's a move afoot to let some of the others play golf at off-peak times at the local club. If you like I could enquire whether you might be allowed to walk over to the shops. There are some quite nice shops not very far away. Thank you, but I've got used to just walking around where I'm supposed to be, studying rocks and stones and flowers and things. It's okay really. Please don't worry.

He gave up in the end — they gave up — because they realised I was harmless, that I contained no vile and plotting thoughts, that I could be relied upon to behave properly. And I did. I did behave properly. I have always behaved properly. For my entire life I've behaved properly — except just that once.

Finally they let me loose in the kitchen and that is how I became such a good cook. Take one mark off for boasting. Nine out of ten. I cook reasonably competently at my best, ordinarily but reliably at my worst.

They mean well. In ordinary conversation that little combination of words has a damning quality. They mean well. How often have you heard it, accompanied by a smirk or a shrug, contemptuous, faintly dismissive. But they did mean well. My interests were noted, just as those of others were noted, and people were brought in to foster those interests. One Christmas, a famous television cook came in to teach me how to make festive chocolates and left the little moulds and everything so I could make the same chocolates for everyone the next Christmas.

People do mean well and you get strangers meaning well, too. Perhaps they might have done what we had done, what I had done, if they had been isolated enough, worried enough, had the opportunity. Perhaps that is what some people think so they offer to help, to pay silently for crimes not committed, but which easily could have been. Perhaps they realise they are equally flawed but have just not been found out yet.

I was not the only one to be chosen for training. If I had been interested in birds like a woman in the next block, they would have brought in an ornithologist to speak to me about the migratory habits of the heron, and others. The director of the nearest museum would have been approached with a view to arranging visits there, in the evening when it was officially closed to the general public, and a selection of suitable books from the museum's private library could have been sent. There was a library where we were and they were happy to buy books on positive subjects, but specialised issues were not well represented. If I had been the one interested in birds, for instance, when I left I would already have been exquisitely and slowly trained — we had plenty of time — in the subtle arts of taxidermy. I would have been quietly integrated, on parole, into the hidden inner chambers of some notable museum to work in stress-free circumstances, mostly alone and in the basement, using knives with short blades on creatures that were already dead.

For pre-parole it was arranged that I would work in a church, not in any religious sense but just doing clerical jobs and other tasks that other people did not have time for. Sometimes I swept all the verandahs, particularly in autumn when a lot of leaves fell. I suppose, I supposed, the authorities arranged this because they thought I was good. I am not good. I am not bad either. I am mediocre. Take another mark off the total for being too hard on yourself again, Stephanie. You are no less good or more bad than anyone else. That is what the man said, the man with the notebook.

I was the one, though, who was given the cooking lessons. They brought in an elderly man called Tony who had once owned a family restaurant on the main road towards the coast and from him I learned the ordinary but delicious arts of roasting beef to faintly pink perfection, rarer if you like, and completely and reliably correlating the timing of cooking vegetables with the meat, not an easy task. He taught me how to present an impeccable baked potato and how to cook asparagus so its texture and colour were perfect by bringing the water to the boil for a scant eight seconds. Tony taught me all that. He also taught me never to cut the woody ends off asparagus but to bend the spears quickly to break off naturally the part that is too tough. Never cut your asparagus, Stephanie, Tony used to say. I'll just take this sharp little paring knife away from you, my dear. Just bend your asparagus like this, and snap — there you have the best part left in your hands. Discard the rest, or add it to the stock for soup. That is what he used to say. I'll just pop this knife away, Stephanie. The really wonderful thing always to keep in mind with cooking asparagus is that a knife is seldom necessary. Asparagus is a truly noble vegetable, Stephanie. Next week we'll get on to julienne carrots and I might have time to touch on the marination of lean lamb.

He meant well. They all meant well. I meant well, years ago, when I climbed in my car and set off northward, the back seat loaded up with the things I judged were too precious for the removal men to handle. I meant very well. I was trying to find another life and I did actually do that. I did find another life but it was not the one I had in mind. No need to take three marks off for failure. The notebook man would say that. It was just not a success in the way I had anticipated.

Four

A LILAC TREE had always grown outside the
seaward windows of the upstairs bedrooms, with heavily scented blooms
of such a luminous shade of deep purple that they seemed improbable.
Its leaves were a bright and springing green in the daylight and at night
lay dark against the bright moon like the bruised marks of many thumbs
on a throat.

*Did you plot where you were to meet him? Did you inveigle him into
your home to trap him? Did you place the knife in that exact drawer with
the idea that you would kill him already in your mind many hours before?
No, indeed. Whenever I thought of what he did to me — you know, the
lies he told me about his wife and how he said she was too delicate ever to
be upset but I could be upset easily any time and no one ever worried
about it or gave a damn, as if I had no feeling or was made of stone — I
used to get a feeling sometimes that I might like to put my hands around
his throat and strangle him. Just to shut him up so I did not have to listen
to this endless litany about his wife and her health and her family who
were all so clever and wonderful and so well placed and could never be
upset, but I could be upset and it didn't ever seem to matter. Yes? And
what next? I used to think it would be logistically impossible to do this
because he was too tall. Is that when you decided to stab him? No, I never
decided to do anything. I didn't know what to do. It all just happened.*

On the dressing table in the front bedroom stood an old gesso lamp,
its base formed by a figurine of a kneeling woman in a red crinoline, her

17

arms outstretched to two spaniels, the painted glaze still pristine after so many years. It had always been a careful house where things were well looked after, where changes in fashion were not noticed greatly, where if an object had been purchased and continued to find favour, it remained in the position for which it had been originally intended. She stretched out her hand for the lamp's switch and the sudden sparkle of light showed her a tide of small objects on the glass surface of the dressing table. All the furniture in the room was oak, a matching suite. It had been there for as long as she could remember. The surface of the dressing table had a piece of plate glass on the top to protect the wood. Through it the old grain glimmered, golden and unstained by the years.

'Goodnight,' she called through the wall to Louise. 'I'll see you in the morning. Everything's going to be fine, you'll see. I might sit and write for a while before I go to sleep, like I said. If you hear me moving around, please don't worry. I'll just be writing.' From the other room there was no sound, no answering voice.

Two ring boxes, one red morocco faded to ox-blood brown and the other bakelite with an oyster-shell pattern, sat beneath the dressing table's wide wing mirror. Both containers had velvet interiors that were pristine but empty, the hinges broken as if they had once, a long time ago, been torn open in a hurry, the jewels quickly grasped and then someone had run away through the house, down the stairs, the footsteps urgent amidst the dust motes. A tarnished silver powder bowl holding the remnants of a broken string of beads sat beside a small, empty, silver picture frame devoid of a backing, its velvet lining faded from mauve to faintest grey like sad, bleached thoughts.

On a large, square, crystal dressing table tray stood four crystal vases of excellent quality, though they were dusty. All were empty of blooms except one, which held two amethyst-headed hat pins shaped like flowers of a mythical breed, a silver and enamel shamrock bracelet and, garlanding the vase's rounded base, an ivory bangle carved with leaves and blossoms. A second silver powder bowl, this one without a lid, contained a small, round, tapestry-embroidered tape measure for a lady's handbag. Her very pale hands, faintly reddened on their backs from the day's intermittent sun as she drove, moved quietly among the items, rearranging them, dusting the cut patterns on the vases with her handkerchief, polishing the enamelled shamrocks of the bracelet till the green came up verdant and beautiful as fields, the tarnish beginning to drop away from the silver links. A long time ago she had kept everything immaculately in her own house and now, idly and almost anonymously, from remembered habit, set about the usual tasks again in her cousin's house.

She went to the window again and looked out. Perhaps, she thought, twenty-five minutes might have gone by. And the leaves against the moon still looked like bruises on a throat.

Would you like to tell us exactly why you did it? No. I have written why I did it very clearly on a piece of paper which one of you must have in one of those folders I can see on the table. If you read the piece of paper you will see exactly why I did it. But why don't you wish to tell us? Why don't you wish to state clearly why you did it? Because, if I did, I would begin to cry and I do not cry in front of strangers. And you still can't tell us what happened to that hour and a half not accounted for? Perhaps I fainted. But you've already said you left immediately, that you set off immediately for the police station. Perhaps I didn't. Perhaps I only thought I did. Perhaps I fainted and then I came down here to the police station.

A photograph in a velvet frame stood on the dressing table. A woman in an Edwardian dress, the hem plainly turned up, the side seams faintly puckered as if the garment had been made laboriously on a hand-operated sewing machine at home with a needle blunted by use, or even sewn by hand entirely and slightly in a hurry, without regard for the finer detail. There was great care, though, in the arrangement of the lace on an overdress, in the neat white cuffs above nearly invisible hands that clutched the back of a carved chair and became lost themselves, like more secrets, among the wooden flowers and grapes emblazoned on the finials and the fretwork pediment. Only strong capable wrists were truly visible, on one of them a stout watch with a dark leather strap and a round innocent face like another eye.

It would be a picture, she thought, of an earlier relative removed by two or three generations and yet they all still bore that air of withdrawal that set them apart, perhaps a family thing ingrained in their faces forever, set even more in the bones and the flesh as they aged. All of them would have been dragged into the world red, bawling and shrieking, slowly becoming, over the next thirty or forty years, pale, withdrawn, so reticent it was commented on by the neighbours.

One or two of the neighbours had come forward. Yes, she had been a very pleasant person in the area. No, she had not caused any trouble. Kept herself to herself, said one old man and then limped away, casting one significant glance behind him as if he reproached them all for the intrusion into his own withdrawal. If she had a fault at all, he said, it was that she was too quiet and sometimes he had wondered if she was there at all or might be ill, so he had gone in through her little picket gate and up over the old verandah of her little cottage with a bag of his very own tomatoes as an excuse to make sure she was there and was all right. No, he had said, he never noticed anything amiss, except the hedge. The hedge? What about the hedge? Well, she was forgetful about the hedge and every year, as the privet bloomed, he had to ask her to trim it because it shaded his greenhouse where he grew the cactus plants he was so fond of, and the tomatoes he had shared with her and where he started off his cos lettuce seedlings, tenderly tucked away in there, warm and sheltered from the wind that sometimes ripped in from the north. But it was just that she didn't think about hedges. She wasn't a lady who would have had hedges on her mind, he said. It wasn't that she was careless or anything like that, not at all. He had been brought up with hedges and thought about them. But she was a lady who didn't think about hedges. She always got it cut right away, as soon as he asked, he said, the voice quick and nearly urgent. There was never any trouble. She was a good neighbour, had been a good neighbour, he corrected himself. She can come back anytime, he said. Anytime. You don't get it that often, not these days, not in the city, a nice, quiet neighbour who'll have the hedge cut when you ask, just like that, with no trouble. That's what I've come to say, he said, and now I've said it. And as for visitors — no, she hadn't ever had many visitors at all, except for just the one man who came to lunch sometimes on a Thursday. Mostly regular as clockwork every Thursday but sometimes not. Yes, that is his picture. That's him. Thank you, sir. We may call upon you again if we need you. Thank you for your time.

Below the windows, past the lilac that was stirring in the wind, she could see that the old hedges in her cousin's garden had been removed in her absence. Wooden fences lined the property now, higher towards the back where the old vegetable garden lay, much diminished in size because these days only Louise lived here and there is a limit to the number of carrots and potatoes, cabbages and lettuces one woman can eat in a season. The old drive had been cobbled, she noticed in the moonlight. The original twin strips of concrete leading to the garage had been pulled up and she thought she could perhaps recognise them all over again as a crazy paving path through the shrubbery that was redolent with more lilacs.

Her own cottage far away in the city had been sold. Perhaps, by now, it had even been demolished to allow for inner-city development, the rose garden she had made there all torn up, the trees felled, no more golden leaves from the liquidambar in autumn tides against the hedge she had been so assiduous about having trimmed when asked to do so, the furniture from inside the place all gone and the picket gate that led to the verandah chopped up for someone's firewood. Another person may now own the chiffonier whose mottled oval mirror once held the ashen image of her own face and the old Persian rug that lay in front of it had been taken away in a plastic bag with a number on it, one of the first things to go.

Only the car had been kept, curiously and mysteriously, by the proprietor of the garage where the vehicle was always serviced. He had come forward, a stalwart, blue-eyed man whom she hardly recognised in a dark suit and a maroon paisley tie. He had always looked like a farmer from down south somewhere, square about the shoulders in his overalls, the sort of man you see driving a tractor along a side road, gesturing the traffic past as he turns into a gateway, the cattle already waiting there patiently for the expected winter feed-out of hay or ensilage loaded on to his trailer, strings of saliva gently dribbling from their jaws in expectation. He had always looked like that, an escapee from a small farm who somehow had a garage in the city and leaned laconically against the doors of cars as their owners told him what they wanted. A general service and check for a long trip, please. An oil change. A warrant of fitness. Something wrong with the gears when you change her into second — have a look at it, Russell, will you? Yet that day in court he had walked into the box, neat and citified in that dark suit and she had not recognised him. It was only the voice that made her look up.

Yes, she had always been an excellent customer. Of all the customers who had ever frequented his garage she had been the most polite, the most tolerant, the kindest and the most thoughtful, the best payer of her modest bills, never a hint of trouble in any way at all. The car was there at the moment to have the carburettor checked, he said. He would do the job and keep the vehicle up on blocks till she needed it again. No, there would not be a charge and yes, he knew it might be a long time. The wheels would have to come off because the tyres would deteriorate, but the whole thing was entirely manageable and was not unusual. People went off to Saudi Arabia and other countries on overseas appointments for three or four years and they didn't want to sell their Porsche or whatever because it was a collector's item. Not that it was a Porsche she had. His voice had become a little hurried then, apologetic, so she looked up again. Perhaps he thought that if they imagined she was wealthy she might be fined as well. It was just an ordinary saloon car but had been kept in good order, immaculate really because she was an immaculate lady and he wanted to tell them that, but it would stand up to storage quite well. Thank you, you may step down now. Please go and sit over there, with the other gentleman. Yes, but before I go I want to say, a lady like that, well, there must have been something that made her do it because she wouldn't have done it if there hadn't been, not someone like that. There must have been something. She was always very good-humoured and the only time she got the least bit impatient was on a Thursday if they were late with her car and even then she was impatient in a nice kind of way. She'd say, Oh hell's teeth, Russell, this is a bit of a bummer — but it isn't your fault, I know that. It's just that I'm expected most urgently elsewhere. That's the way she talked. You have been asked to sit down. Please join the other gentleman on the seats to the left. So she had watched him go across the room and sit down beside the old neighbour, the one with the hedge.

'Russell, are you quite sure you're not really a farmer?' she used to ask sometimes while he totted up the bill. 'You look so very much like

22

the farmer's sons from down south, where I come from. Are you quite, quite sure? Well, it must be a trick of resemblance through genetics somehow, Russell. Thank you very much,' she would say, handing him the cheque while he told her no, he came from further north and his father had been an accountant in Kaitaia and they'd never had a farm, none of them, not ever in their lives.

He had an internal office, built within the framework of the high arched ceiling of his garage, which had been designed for another purpose a long time ago. From this inner elevated hut, on poles so it had to be approached up a flight of small wooden stairs, Russell organised the car repairs. The building was too narrow for some of the work done on the larger cars, which were taken out on to the street for final titivations. There she always found her own car parked sideways under the nearest tree when she went to collect it. Everything okay, Russell? She seems fine, Mrs Beaumont. We've just given her a bit of a tune-up and the boys have altered the mix. I think you'll find she's quicker off the mark now. Thank you, Russell. Not at all. My pleasure. In the beginning, when she first moved to the city, he always called her Mrs Beaumont, as if she were old, she often thought.

Russell's garage had a system of collection and delivery of vehicles that needed servicing, but she had never asked for this because her car seemed so ordinary in there among the Porsches and the BMWs. She always just telephoned for an appointment to bring it in herself. Hello, Russell, it's me again. Russell, the car's kind of coughing at the traffic lights when I need to get away quickly. Could there be a tube somewhere blocked up, do you think? Pop her in, Mrs Beaumont, and we'll take a peek. Make it two tomorrow. Bring her in at two. While they worked on it she went up the road a few blocks to a nearby library and read books she usually did not have time to study, returning to the garage on foot in the late afternoon. Everything all right, Russell? She's going great. The key's on the hook by my office door. And he would nod his head laconically in the direction of the inner hut. Thank you, Russell, see you next time. Okay then, Mrs Beaumont. See how she goes. Give me a bell if there's anything wrong. He would put a large, strong hand on the bonnet with an almost proprietorial air. She's a great little car and she's in good shape. She'll last another ten years, no sweat. He had divined, somehow, that she worried about things, about everything, that

23

she knew secretly that, when the car died, she would not be able to afford another one. Thank you, Russell. You're very kind. Sometime or another, she could not remember exactly when, he had started giving her credit and sent her a bill the month following the repairs instead of computing it when she arrived and waiting for her to write the cheque or count out the money from her purse. And, perhaps at the same time, he had begun to call her by her Christian name. Thank you, Russell. Cheerio, Stephanie, see ya.

From the high, gabled bedroom window of her cousin's house she looked down again at the car. In the morning she and Louise would open up the doors of the big shed out the back and would rearrange things so there was space to shut the car away like another secret in lives full of such things, the doors closing against glances from the curious. The car, as if sensing the secrecy, sat darkly beneath the high and spreading branches of a gingko tree, as far away from the street as she had been able to park it.

Last week's announcement about her proposed release had been very discreet, though, and had attracted little interest, making only page five of one of the main metropolitan newspapers and had been discarded by the rest as being possibly too out-of-date, too dull. One or two of the provincials had run it, one on its leader page as a little panel with a fancy black outline, but mostly it had not made any more than a paragraph or two.

The building from which Russell ran his garage business must once have been a laundry, she remembered now, the high arched double doors at the front designed to accommodate the bulk of laundry trucks bearing bundles of washing. There had been the name of a company set into the cement above the arch, painted over so it was not clearly visible but still printed on the stone architrave. As she climbed into the big oak bed she tried to recall what the name was, the words that were written into the cement on that pale blue façade made of old pebbledash rough-cast, never originally designed to discourage graffiti but, she remembered, most peculiarly effective against vandalism.

I've escaped again. There would be Russell smiling outside the garage when she arrived in the bedaubed street. They've been out overnight, Russell, I see. Indeed they have, but they can't write on me, Stephanie, because I'm too rough. And there he would be, grinning in front of the old laundry façade. Always, in her infinite games of minuscule recollection, the name written on that façade eluded her.

As an exercise to put herself to sleep, she had invented a process of total and fond recall of things never properly regarded at the time, so she had often conjured up the vision of Russell outside the old laundry building on a fine morning long ago, her car awaiting attention and the sun shining down upon them all. She had, in her own mind, gone over each pebble, each stone of that facade, as she lay waiting to go to sleep at night for months, for years. Her vision always showed her the old garage with its doors folded back, the small window of what might once have been a laundry manager's little room at the front, now demolished to make room for the cars, the tiny window high up and seemingly haphazard and looking down as Russell dished out the day's work to the men. Just take a peek at Mrs Beaumont's car will you, Charlie? She says she's slow off at the lights. Have a look at the mixture.

In her cousin's house she now lay under the fluff of white blankets and again tried to remember the name set in cement and written above those doors. From far away down the stairs, past where the old dolls' pram used to be, came the sound of the grandfather clock striking two in the morning.

Five

'YOU WERE UP late last night. Couldn't you sleep?' That was Louise, standing in the doorway with a cup of tea in her hand. If the town had been larger there might have been some sound of early morning traffic coming from the road outside, but the silence seemed enduring from the garden and the trees. Rush hour used to be later, at eight o'clock sharp, thought Stephanie, and took five minutes to pass, except for Fridays when it took six. 'I saw your light shining out over the trees till all hours. I woke up at one in the morning by my clock and you still had your light on.' Louise came across the room and stood by the bed, one side of her dressing gown hanging loose. 'You'll have to help me with this, I'm sorry. I can't get my arm in. And you didn't lock your door.'

Glazed by sleep, Stephanie sat up slowly from the shroud of the bed, swinging her legs over the side. The floral carpet had been there as long as she could remember, its roses and bluebells dimmed only a little by the years.

'No, don't get up. It's too early. I just want you to help me with this.' Louise flapped the dressing gown. 'I'm sorry to be a nuisance.' She put the cup of tea on a small round table beside the bed, the china roses on the cup suddenly nearly lurid against the black-stained wood.

'You're not a nuisance. This is what I came for. I came to look after you.' She sat on the edge of the bed, slowly regarding the problem of the dressing gown and Louise and the two arms, one healed a long time ago and the other held close to the chest, the stitches still new and as yet unseen. 'I think we'll just slip this off' — she slowly slid the sleeve off

Louise's good arm and began all over again — 'and if we carefully put the bad arm in first, and I slip the sleeve up over it so you don't have to bend it or move it, then you can move your good arm,' she said, 'to go in that other sleeve. There you are, Louise. All done. That's a much better way of doing it.' She took the cup of tea. 'Do you always have tea early in the morning? Whatever's the time?'

'It's just after six. I like to have a cup of tea and then I go out and look at the garden. I like to see what's happened overnight.'

They had always been great ones for their boundaries, she thought, her feet still planted squarely on a pink carpet rose. They had been a family that was parochial about land, about possession, about property. Like the air of withdrawal that became slowly ingrained in their very flesh, the idea of their property, whatever it might be, was enmeshed in their minds and was always mentioned by family members in conjunction with their names. Uncle Tom who's got a block of flats. Auntie Mary who's got a string of race horses. Uncle John who's got a farm. Granny who retired to town on a piece of land that Uncle Ken gave her to build a cottage on when she left her farm. Their property, however small, was like oxygen in their nostrils but they still died, one after another, of the usual causes, just like everyone else, even though they were inordinately fond of their belongings, were proud of owning things. Uncle Tom had once had a professional photograph taken of his block of flats, a bland and featureless building, and had included it in his Christmas cards.

'Uncle Tom,' she said, the voice careful, studied. Her sleep had been so final and so deep and the awakening had been so sudden that there was a need for conscious clarity. 'Tell me what happened to Uncle Tom. If he were alive he'd be very old now, wouldn't he?' She took a sip of the tea, cool now after its journey from the kitchen at the back of the house, up the stairs, into the front bedroom. It was a house of architectural and personal distances, where the people stayed apart, preserved their own space, did not reveal themselves.

'He died years ago. You must remember.' Louise stopped speaking so suddenly that Stephanie realised, equally suddenly, that they must both have thought, in the same instant, of where she had been and how you do not get news there, or not a lot and, even though people might write, they might forget to say some things. How are you? The weather has been good lately. We have had a good summer. I hope you are keeping well. Did you get the bundle of old *Time* magazines I had finished with and that I sent you back in the winter? That was the kind of thing people wrote. After the first two or three years the only letters she received had been from Louise and yet, in real life before that, they had scarcely ever been in contact at all for a long time. Perhaps their own self-imposed isolation, this family trait of privacy, prompted Louise to think it was then perfectly safe to write to her, to be friendly, because she could never be a nuisance on the doorstep, because she was far away in every possible way. Last time we were talking, Louise would write, I told you about the terrible storm we had a couple of months ago. The old lilac tree was bent over nearly to the ground and I thought it would break off in the force of the wind. They were such a family for silence, for their passionate, personal silences, that, after a year or two, Louise had begun to refer to the letters as talking and, such was their reticence, the silent words on notepaper were possibly, to her, as vivid as real conversation.

It's nice to have someone to talk to, Louise wrote in her round, careful hand. I sometimes find it a bit lonely in this big house by myself since Mother died. Perhaps she had just not thought to say, or write, that Uncle Tom had died. The two terms became muddled in her own mind. Say. Write. Uncle Tom never wrote but then he never had written letters. None of them wrote, except Louise. The family distance was strong in them all. Her recollections of him, of them all, unremittingly involved distance. A seated figure over by the bay window in his house, silently playing cribbage — was it cribbage? — by himself. Here comes Uncle Tom. Children, all be good, please. A view of a distant figure coming in the gate. Wave to Uncle Tom, children. Did you have a nice time at Uncle Tom's? It was very good of him to let you play in the garden. I hope you said thank you. And afternoon tea as well? Snax biscuits with tomato on? And an orange drink? What a lucky girl.

'What made you think of Uncle Tom? I haven't thought of Uncle Tom for years. I wouldn't have thought you knew him very well.'

'I didn't. He just somehow came into my mind, oddly, in the early morning.'

'I think he died about four or five years ago, I've forgotten the exact year. He was very old and he had a stroke and then he died a few days later. Anyway, I must go down and see the garden.' Louise turned slowly, her good arm guarding the other, the silk of the dressing gown fluttering slightly. It was as much hurry as she could manage, thought Stephanie. If she had been perfectly well she might even have run away from the human being who suddenly tenanted the best room, a creature who had made a dent in a mattress that for years had been smooth with its own coverings of satin quilts and ruched bedspreads. 'Go back to sleep. I'll have to get you to help me have a bath later, but we'll talk about it after breakfast. There's plenty of time. It's very early. I always wake up very early. It's hours till we need to think about the bath.' She went out the door in that slight flurry of silk again, possibly propelled by the idea of this ultimate invasion of herself. 'Perhaps I wouldn't need to have a bath today at all, do you think? Could we leave it till tomorrow?' Her voice, coming from the upstairs landing, possessed a quality of dedicated reticence, like something from a foreign radio station. The footsteps retreated, then returned.

'I didn't ask,' she said from the doorway, 'do you like it? Is it all right?'

'Is what all right?' Through the partially open door out on to the landing she could see just half of Louise now — one foot, one shoulder, one eye downcast, the rest hidden by the door jamb. Like crustaceans, she thought, they did not come completely out of their crepuscular casings till they were sure of a welcome, even in their own homes and with their own kind.

'The table. Is the table all right? I put it beside your bed yesterday when I got home. It's the one I usually have in my own room. I thought you might need a table beside your bed. While I waited for you I put a few things in your room that you might need. I got everything ready for you.'

Stephanie climbed out of bed then, gave up the loving clasp of the quicksand mattress and walked right to the door.

'Louise,' she said, 'that was very kind of you. It's a beautiful table. It's a beautiful room. I love it. It was very good of you to get it all ready for me, do believe me. And, never forget,' she said, going too far as she sometimes did, and not caring, 'never forget, Louise, that you were a very beautiful girl. I remember you when you were grown up and I was just a little girl and I thought you were the most beautiful girl I'd ever seen —'

'You haven't seen me properly now.' Louise was leaning against the banisters now, her face turned away.

'— and,' she said, 'you're still beautiful, no matter what's happened, you're still beautiful. And thank you for the table. And the tea.' They both padded away, barefooted, in their separate directions, Louise down the stairs, Stephanie back to the bed, the pair of them fleeing from the luxuriance of compliments, of clearly stated regard, from the affliction of affection.

So, thought Stephanie leaning back on the reclaimed pillows, sinking again into the tender grip of that mattress, Louise had deliberately got the room ready for her yesterday, and today the bath was going to be a problem.

She lay there, charting Louise's progress through the house. The stairs had always creaked faintly. Now there was silence for a moment or two while Louise stopped on the middle landing. A high window let light into the stairwell there and beneath this, where the dolls' pram used to stand, a long oak footstool had been placed. It had tapestry upholstery — embroidered huntsmen in cross-stitch red coats with black and white dogs on a fine morning. Louise, she thought, might be standing on this to look down at her vegetable garden.

The letters, over the years, had contained many references to the garden. My gerberas have come on a real treat since I started using the liquid manure. I notice that when people are out for a walk in the evening they often stop and look over my fence to see my flowers. The corn is doing well and has set eighteen cobs, which I am looking forward to eating when they are ready. I have a good crop of lettuces.

The creaking resumed and then, from the entrance hall, came a curious whirring noise that she could not place for a moment. The weights on the grandfather clock, she thought at last. Louise was pulling up the weights of the clock on their chains because, while she was in hospital, they must slowly have nearly reached the bottom of the case. The clock would stop any day now if the weights were not pulled up to the top again. After that there was the sound of a door opening and closing, then silence. Louise had gone out to the back wing of the house, to her kitchen and the teapot and her own private thoughts, her own cup of tea drunk in her own incomparable solitude while she looked out over what was left of the old garden.

A trellis fence divided the back area, only briefly glimpsed the previous evening in the gloom of dusk, the sights as still and silent as photographs. A row of rhubarb plants flourishing against a stone wall. A new apple tree planted in the middle of the lawn, its label fluttering. A big daisy bush, rampant with large flowers like faces. A few herbs planted within the framework of an old wagon wheel lying on the ground, some segments left empty but well tilled. It was rusty but quaint, perhaps a remnant of one of the old family farms. Uncle Tom had once had a farm, before he owned the block of flats. The old hen houses had gone, and were replaced by a neat vegetable garden in which Louise was growing corn in circles, so that each plant supported the next one, and cucumbers in a wire frame so they grew upwards instead of untidily outwards, the fruit, she hoped, hanging cleanly away from the soil and more easily pickable. Louise would be out there, all alone, regarding her property as the sun came up and people began to drive down the road to work.

The sound of traffic now began to come faintly through the upstairs windows, as if everyone who had ever lived in the house wished to hear the resonances and cadences of strangers only from a very great distance, muffling them with the stoutest wood, the thickest velvet, the rosiest floral carpets. People were driving past the old house set in all the trees, the blinds pulled down on its gabled windows like closed eyes. The quality of light in the house was quite different from her memory of it. Once the sun had slanted down the stairs from open bedroom doors, from casements flung wide, lace curtains fluttering in breezes from the margins of the sea. Now the doors were closed darkly and locked, the rooms becoming sudden mysteries, the upstairs landing and the staircase engulfed in endless, shuttered evening. She had placed her own cold hand on each knob in turn the previous night and each time it was the same. Locked. The best sitting room at the front of the house, the old dining room where they used to roll up the carpet and dance, all the bedrooms upstairs except Louise's old room and this front bedroom she had been given — they were all locked.

When the silence from downstairs became impenetrable and the sun began to shine through the narrow window of her bedroom, she got up at last and, pushing the casement open, leaned out to feel the fresh air, to judge the strengths and weaknesses of the day. It was peculiar, she thought, to be able to do such a simple thing after all this time. To open the window and lean out seemed a miraculous exercise, so privately pleasurable that it was almost painful. Down the road, a few blocks away,

31

was the sea and the light breeze blowing inland had brought with it a faint tang of salt, a crisp feeling of freshness from the shore.

Time to go downstairs, she thought, and listened to the creaking of the old stair treads under her own bare feet as she went quietly through the old house. The footstool gave an excellent view of the vegetable garden. That is why Louise must have put it there, she thought. It would be a while before the corn was ready. No sign of cucumbers forming on the vines but there were numerous flowers so that was a good sign.

From far away she could hear the flick-clack of a helicopter and, when she went to find Louise in the kitchen she suddenly stood there, beside the new stove, and could think of nothing to say that was suitable for a fine, sunny morning with the birds singing outside and the combined mysteries of all the locked doors to consider.

'I heard a Hughes earlier,' she said quite wildly in her own odd way, a rage of shyness that no one ever divined.

'I beg your pardon?' Louise looked up from the morning paper.

' A Hughes. A Hughes helicopter. I heard a Hughes helicopter earlier. It must have been spraying crops somewhere.' The silence lengthened. 'It's quite windy today so they'll be using a wide mesh on the sprayer so the stuff doesn't go everywhere.' The silence continued. 'On still days they use a fine mesh.' Louise continued to stare at her, over the top of the newspaper, absolutely motionless.

'There's a big tomato farm just up the road,' she said at last. 'They'll be doing that, I suppose.' So the revelation of one of Stephanie's curious pieces of knowledge was dragged back into the realm of ordinary conversation. In the end she had been sent to a low security establishment out in the country where the buzzing of small topdressing aircraft and the flick-clack of the helicopter rotors somehow gave a rhythm to thoughts. Flick-clack. It was inevitable, it wasn't inevitable. I'm sorry, I'm not sorry. I'm sorry I did it because I ruined my life, but I'm not sorry ultimately that I did it. Flick, clack.

'Doing what?' she said.

'Spraying the tomatoes. Like you just said. About the helicopter.' Louise regarded her with care, lowering the newspaper now.

'Of course. My mind was just elsewhere for a moment. Of course we were talking about the tomato place.' Take a mark off for not keeping track of things, another mark off for loss of lucidity. Eight out of ten. 'I'm sorry, Louise.'

'Perhaps we could drive up there and see if they've got any for sale.' Louise, newspaper in hand, was now captured by the idea of tomatoes. 'There's nothing nicer than a fresh tomato sandwich, is there, Steph —' The telephone had begun to ring, a muffled shrill from the foot of the stairs in a house where the doors were very thick and seemed now to be mostly bolted. 'I'd better go and answer that,' she said. 'They said they'd ring every morning.' Her voice, when she picked up the telephone, was measured, plausible, ingenuous and calm, cutting clearly through the still air with a sibilant innocence.

Yes, everything was very quiet. Her cousin Stephanie — Stephanie Beaumont, yes that was her full name — had arrived, as scheduled, just before dinner the previous evening. She had said the drive was pleasant and uneventful. No, she had not said anything about stopping on the way for any length of time and, judging by the time, she had not done so. They were going to have breakfast together in the kitchen right now. Perhaps tomorrow, depending on how she felt and what the doctor said she could do, they might drive to the tomato gardens up the road to buy some fresh vegetables. Stephanie would have to drive but she was always a good driver and would be able to get the hang of Louise's car in a moment. No, if they went out Louise wanted her own car driven, not Stephanie's, in case the battery went flat. It was a red Mazda, last year's model. Stephanie listened to the recitation of the registration number. Yes, Louise knew it was confusing but it couldn't be helped. Stephanie had been very helpful so far and a little drive up the road, only half a mile or so, wouldn't do anyone any harm, would it? No, she couldn't remember the name of the gardens. And no, they weren't new gardens. They had been there for years. And yes, owned by the same family. You know what it's like — you deal at a place for years and you don't ever properly know its name, you just call it that nice place with the red roof or something like that? And she didn't know exactly what time they'd be going because it depended on a lot of things like the weather and how they felt and they mightn't even go at all. You know what women are like about changing their minds. Thank you. Goodbye.

'Sorry about that. It's just a little call I'll have to answer every day.' Louise had returned to the kitchen, the hall door slamming crisply behind her like something snapped shut on an unpleasant thought. There was another of those long pauses. 'I think we'll definitely have tomato sandwiches for lunch tomorrow, after we've been up to the gardens. I've suddenly quite set my heart on fresh tomatoes,' she said. She had picked up the newspaper again. 'And fancy you knowing all about helicopters.'

A greyness had come over the day, obscuring the brilliant early morning, but it had always been an area like that, where the weather changed quickly from one hour to another. Her idea that her own sudden rising sense of desolation even marked the weather and the universe was ridiculous.

'It'll come out fine again in an hour or so, you'll see,' said Louise, as if she had divined this thought. 'And I feel much better today. Perhaps, later, we could walk around the garden together. I've done a quick circuit myself but you could come with me and I'll show you the weeds,' and Stephanie watched her give one of those wry grins that were a kind of family thing as well, perhaps another pattern stained in their flesh.

Six

THE HOUSE WAS a place of unfathomable recollection. The stairs were covered now in white plush carpet, but the old pink roses and bluebells of the floral runner that once wound up to the top floor lay in her mind like a myth, the difference between recollection and reality almost a shock. A remnant of the rosy carpet, perhaps the only good piece left, had been placed beside the bed in the front room, a bouquet of flowers to hold her thin adult feet.

You've been told a thousand times, Stephanie, that you're not to run up the stairs. Next time you'll have to be smacked. The dolls are not yours, and you're not allowed to play with them. Small, determined feet going downstairs now, hopping from one bluebell to another, now a rose, tripping on the brass clips that held the carpet in place at the edge of each step. There you are — that's what happens to naughty little girls. They trip and hurt themselves. It serves you right. Please don't squeeze my hand like that, it hurts. I'm squeezing your hand, Stephanie, to make you understand what a naughty, naughty girl you are and I'm just squeezing your hand so you'll know, Stephanie. Please don't open the door into the hall again, Stephanie, or there's going to be trouble. Stay in the kitchen. Please be a good girl. I've got enough to worry about without you as well.

A scalloped brocade curtain, the colour of dead leaves, had once always been drawn over the high window designed to light the stairwell, the dolls in their pram lying in a state of perpetual shade beneath it, every pair of big blue eyes closed against each motionless and uninterrupted day. Now the light fell brightly and sharply through the small bare panes, the only direct sunlight in the upper part of the house, and the stool that stood in the pram's place gave an enveloping view of the back garden. She stepped up there again and stood for a moment like an old child viewing illicit sights. Next door, through the trees, someone was hanging washing on a clothesline. From further away came the sound of a lawnmower. The brass hooks that had once held the curtain were still screwed firmly into the wood of the window's architrave and, on top of the carved pelmet, she could feel, with the same exploring hand that had found the locked doors, the old tiebacks made of faded silk cord and perhaps placed there for possible further use.

'One of these days, I'm going to get more curtains made for there.' Louise stood in the entrance hall, looking up through the dust motes. 'I've kept all that, just in case.' None of them ever wasted anything. 'We could find the same kind of material and get them made somewhere.' She went back into the kitchen, leaving the door open behind her.

'There's the matter of the bath to be thought about.' Stephanie, from her elevated position on top of the stool, waited for some kind of answer from the back of the house. The door at the foot of the stairs was wide open so she felt certain Louise would have heard this edict, with everything it signified. Nakedness, revelation, invasion, disclosure, all that. 'The bath,' she repeated, her voice filtering down the stairwell with a peculiar authority, like the sound of a speaking statue. Motionless, she waited on the stool. They were a very specialised and peculiar breed, she thought, unable to mention baths to each other unless they were in separate parts of the house, even deliberately standing in an elevated position to give an illusion of authority.

'I thought I'd leave it till tomorrow.' Louise had returned to the doorway now and stood gazing at the grandfather clock. 'I think the clock needs winding,' she said.

'No, it doesn't. You did it earlier. I heard you pull the weights up after you brought me that cup of tea. It won't need anything more now, not till at least Friday.' She waited. 'It's a five-day clock, as I recall.' Once again she waited. 'You can get very grubby getting in and out of taxis.' She made it sound like an enticement. 'Didn't you come home from the hospital in a taxi?' Years ago, when they were both children, their mothers had endlessly scrubbed bus seats with crumpled lace handkerchiefs before they were allowed to sit down, later wiping their faces with other embroidered squares of cambric drawn from capacious black leather handbags that smelt faintly of face powder and perfume.

Have you got a clean handkerchief, Stephanie? I think so. Stephanie, thinking so is no good. I'll ask you again, have you got a clean handkerchief? Nice little girls don't go out without a clean hanky. I'll go and get one for you. And please always remember to wipe the bus seat with your hanky before you sit down. You never know who's sat there before you. Stephanie, are you listening?

One of their silences lengthened again. 'I do think it might be a good idea to just sit for a moment or two in a couple of inches of hot water,' she said. 'You wouldn't really even need any soap.' She was becoming desperate now, making the bath into something that was not exactly a bath, transforming it into a mere wet chair. 'And I could shut my eyes and help you in and out without looking. But, I mean, Louise, we're all old now, none of it really matters.' Louise was looking fixedly at the clock. The ticking seemed determined.

'All right,' said Louise at last, 'but I don't like the water too hot. I've got a very sensitive skin. And not till I've had another cup of tea and had my breakfast and read the mail.'

So, thought Stephanie from the dolls' position on the landing, we've got that far. Five out of ten.

'The mail usually comes quite early.' Louise loitered down by the clock. 'Someone might have sent me a card, you never know. If the power bill's come I'll have to write out the cheque straightaway or I might forget. I'd hate to have the power cut off.'

'I'll go and have a look.' She was stepping neatly off the footstool now, giving up the glimpse of the garden, of the tailored corn cobs, the rhubarb by the trellis. 'And then I'll get your breakfast and then I'll start running your bath.'

'But if anyone's sent me a card or anything, if something's come in the mail, I'll have to give them a ring to thank them right away. I don't think I'll write any letters for a while. But after that, when I've made sure all that's attended to and when I've had my toast, then I might have a little bath. But not too hot, mind. And only a couple of inches of water, nothing too deep.' Louise turned to go out to the kitchen again, then stopped. 'I'd forgotten about that taxi,' she said. 'Thank you for reminding me. Yes, of course I'd better have a bath.'

Stephanie, if you set some kind of course it isn't always necessary to charge at it headlong and bash your own head to pieces on the figurative wall of the final result. A truly clever person, a wily person if you like, decides on needs and wants with regard to the mores of modern society and works out the least painful way of accomplishing them. Now that man, Stephanie — let us say he had enraged you once too often and you wanted, blindly, to strike back at him. Okay, having a gutsful is not a scientific term, Stephanie, but if you say you'd had a gutsful then I suppose I must acknowledge that you had indeed had, as you put it, a gutsful. You could have damaged him so much more easily and much less distressingly for yourself if you had merely — well, let us consider what you could have done within the realm of what I have said. You could have told his wife. The resulting mayhem in the marriage would have upset his own life in many ways, emotionally and financially. Yes, I realise you would have been considered a cat — but what are you considered now, Stephanie? Might it have been better to be a cat, do you think? If what you've told me is correct, about how he had been given land by the wife's parents, then possibly you could have told them — if you couldn't bring yourself to approach the wife. You could have told them he had had an association with you for some years and you were concerned about your future, you could have said you were concerned about the wife's health, something like that. You could have asked if she was in fact as ill as he claimed. The answer, I think, would have been no. If you had told her, Stephanie, and she had chucked him out, do excuse the colourful expression, then he would have been homeless, Stephanie, just like you were because you hadn't really ever properly bonded with your house in the city, had you? So you were, emotionally speaking, homeless. You had given up your old home and had gone to live in the city, hadn't you, and then you stayed there because of this other man, because of his promises. So, in your own mind, you were homeless, weren't you. Is that what you thought? What an excellent revenge that would have been, if you wanted revenge.

You just wanted to know where you were? You didn't want revenge?
Okay then, so you didn't want revenge. I would have given that nine out
of ten, anyway, simply because, by so doing, you would have saved your-
self. So okay, there would have been a row. So okay, it would have been
unpleasant. Still nine out of ten. So okay, your link with this man would,
thus, have ended. So okay, you might very well have met someone else,
someone better. As it is, Stephanie, or was, sadly I must give you only one
mark, mythologically speaking, which doesn't mean I don't understand
where you were coming from or where you were at or that I don't like you
because you're actually one of my favourite visitors. We never say
patients, Stephanie. Here we use the word visitors. You are one of my
favourite visitors. Also, there is the business of credit, Stephanie. I hesi-
tate to revert to the terminology of gangsterism, but if you had slugged
him in the pocket — If you had got in touch with the proper authorities,
his erstwhile parents-in-law, as it were, and had told them about his emo-
tionally illegal use of their credit facilities, by that I mean their land,
whilst he posed as their devoted son-in-law and had you tucked away on
the side there would have been one hell of a row — and that is a term we
must never officially use because it is denigratory and soils us as much as
it soils him, so I'm right off the record here. Even if you'd packed your-
self up and gone off somewhere for a long holiday to think about it all. You
had nowhere to go? And no money? What was that you said? It was a bit
of a bummer? Yes indeed, Stephanie, it was. It was a bummer all right.

'Oh good,' she said again. 'You don't need to stay in the water long.
I'll put so little in that it wouldn't be enough to drown a fly. You can just
hop in and out in a moment. Just to have a little freshen-up. Just to
please me.'

Never, in all your dealings with people, Stephanie, ever consider the
use of moral blackmail. Take two marks off for this. What's your total for
the day so far? About nil? Take another mark off for being too hard on
yourself. But add two marks for honesty, Stephanie. Your honesty is dis-
tressing but admirable. I feel it should be recognised in some way, but
only as a one-off thing just for today, Stephanie. I can't make a precedent
of this. The tissues are in the third drawer from the left. Perhaps you
would like to go back to your room now, would you?

In the evening they sat on either side of the new table down in the kitchen, the recollection of the old ways of doing things so fresh and so valid that she had made errors in cooking the dinner. The old stove had been green enamel, on cabriole legs, with a large heavy door. When you opened that door the heat and the weight were fierce. The new stove was on the other side of the room, brilliant white, its door so light that her sudden crushing grip on its handle seemed ridiculous.

'How delicious.' Louise began to eat the dinner. 'Where did you learn to do this?'

'They taught me.' It seemed best not to state exactly what, or where, to retreat into generalities. 'I mean, I was taught.'

'Oh.' It was a sharp little sound, again like a door closing. Louise turned to look out one of the new windows, lower than the old one had been, probably more practical, Stephanie thought, yet her own nostalgia about the house's original kitchen had been both fond and comprehensive. At night, unable to sleep, she had silently recalled her last sight of that room, perhaps when she was at a gawky, gangly age, too old for the dolls on the landing and more interested in sitting in the kitchen listening to the radio and the desultory adult talk of the house.

Vera's new husband has bought her a real squirrel coat. Can you believe it? The voices would be hushed with respect for the expense. They all loved money. The wedding was a quiet affair at the registry office. Vera just wore a tailored suit but she had a lovely hat and an orchid corsage and at least he'd married her in the end. We must all hope for the best. She'd had a long wait but the problem had been the old mother. He'd had to wait till his old mother died. Why did he have to wait till the old mother died, she had wanted to know, and whose mother was it anyway, and why? To get the shop, stupid, they had said. He wouldn't get the shop till his old mother died and his old mother wouldn't have Vera at any price because Vera — They had stopped there. Vera had had a chequered history, said an older cousin with a wise and wary look. But she was a nice girl really, a nice woman, and they all wished her luck because she'd need it. Vera had always been good-hearted, too good-hearted for her own good, they said. Vera was golden-hearted. There wasn't a bad bone in her body, it was just that she was too generous and good-hearted with herself. Uncle Tom had given her a cut crystal whisky decanter with six matching tumblers for a wedding present and someone else had sent a cheque for fifty pounds to buy a really nice dinner set, something she'd like and that she could choose herself to match the curtains in her new home and two cousins from the old farm had clubbed together to buy her a silver tray, a silver salver on legs, they said, as if that made it better, which it probably did, even though the cousins had never used a silver salver in their lives. And little pitchers have big ears so we'd better watch what we say. An uncle had built a new shed on his farm, said someone quickly with palpitating innocence. Prices for stock were up. Things were improving. It'll be a better year, you'll see. And don't be cheeky, her mother said that night when they put themselves to bed in the old back room upstairs. Auntie said you were cheeky in the kitchen today. Just mind your P's and Q's and don't pipe up. Sit up and shut up, that's my motto and you'd do yourself a bit of good if you learned it too, madam. It's time you got a few corners knocked off.

The new kitchen windowsill was a narrow strip of aluminium, impossible to arrange anything on at all except, perhaps, a hair clip. The old sill had held two empty glass milk bottles containing assorted rubber bands and carpet tacks, a blue plastic comb, a plant pot with a moribund geranium, a spare set of car keys for a pre-war Morris that had been sold when she had been about eight years old, a photograph of a thin, anxious woman walking along an unidentifiable street clutching the hand of a small child about to cry, various knitting needles — none of them a true pair — some sprigs for golf shoes, a few newspaper clippings headed 'How To Prune Your Roses' and 'New Home For City Club' and a tattered note, written in purple indelible pencil, which read 'Ring Bob about the dog'. After the lights went out, during the long nights, she had gone through it all in her mind so often that it was difficult to know what she truly remembered and what she might have seen elsewhere and transported to the myth of the windowsill. The sill in the bathroom had always been the same. It contained a row of cakes of soap in various colours.

'I look too ugly.' Louise's hands clasped over the buttons of her dressing gown suddenly looked very large and square, and very capable, as the hot water drizzled into the old bath. 'When I'm better,' said Louise with the sudden brightness of those who wish to change the subject, 'I'm going to get this bathroom all done up. I want Italian tiles, but it's a matter of finding exactly the right colour and would I want them hand-painted? Or just plai —'

'Louise, just let me give you a hand with those buttons.' From downstairs came the scent of burnt toast. 'Tomorrow morning, when I make the toast, I must remember to turn that knob back to four. I think five on that particular toaster is too fierce' — her own fingers were on the buttons now, the top one, the second — 'for that light wholemeal bread. It might be all right for rye. Tomorrow we'll turn it back to four and see how we go. If we get rye bread later in the week we must remember to put the knob back on five.' Babble babble. *If you want someone to do something, Stephanie, it's always wise to keep the conversation on some very ordinary soothing subject, keep the pace right down and the stress gets taken out of the situation. Nine out of ten.* 'My goodness me, Louise, there you are now, all undone. Just slip the dressing gown down over those shoulders like so, and hop carefully in. I'll hold your arm so you don't slip.'

'But I look too ugly.' The hands were back at the neck of the dressing gown, clutching the edges together just as the stitches and strappings of surgical tape were holding the edges of the incision beneath that gown. But those were surgical cuts, neat and clean across Louise's chest, up and under the arm, the breast taken away in the tailoring. Her own use of a knife on flesh had been sudden and untutored, years of jointing Number 8 supermarket chickens no training for it. The recollection of it was vile, the nightmares endless, rivalling the childhood ones about money.

I know you've got something hidden away, Stephanie, something Uncle gave you. If you don't give it to me I'll have to get out the razor strap. And there would be her father's big hand held out, a hand that stamped a dark bruise on pale flesh and seemed so large that the mark of it was etched on her brain, the black stains invisible there but the recollection enduring. Give it to him, her mother would say. It's not worth the argument. What do you dream about? That was one of the notebook men, years later. Do you have recurring dreams? I dream about — She stopped there. I dream of nothing specific, she said. Her father's heavy tread and the faint tinkle of the metal ring of the razor strap as it was lifted from its hook in the bathroom might be difficult to explain. So nothing bothers you? said the man with the notebook. Why should it? She lifted one languid shoulder. The appointment ended.

'I look much too ugly.' That was Louise again, hands still at the neck of the gown.

'No, you don't. You look just fine. Just slip this off.' Best not to use the term 'dressing gown'. The anonymous word 'this' might be better. It could mean anything and cause no alarm. 'Come on, I'll hold your hand, just like this, and you can step gently in the bath now. One step. Then another. There's a good girl. The water won't sting. It's just lovely and warm and I'm sure the soap's very mild.' Nurse-like, she bent over the bath with one hand on her own forehead.

It's the usual procedure, they had said. It's the same for everyone. It's part of the regular routine. We inspect the hair just like this. It only takes a moment. Nothing to worry about with yours, but sometimes we find an odd little visitor or two. And you must sit in this bath for exactly four minutes. Yes, it does sting. A lot of people complain about that. You may find the disinfectant causes a slight skin allergy, which will probably pass in a few days. If you just sit there quietly the stinging usually wears off. No, I'm afraid I can't leave you here by yourself. It's just regulations. I have to stay here all the time. I'll just stand over here by the door and if you wouldn't mind passing me your hair slides — you won't be need-ing those after you've had your hair cut. You didn't know you'd have to have your hair cut? It's just regulations again, nothing to worry about. The barber usually comes in late in the afternoon so you can keep all that long hair for a little while longer but I'll have to keep the hair slides, I'm afraid. Why? Because they're quite sharp, aren't they? It's just regula-tions. Nothing to worry about.

'If you'd like me to,' she said, 'I could take you to have a haircut. It might be good for morale, to have your hair done.'

'I haven't had my hair done for ages, not for weeks.' She watched the chin lift a little, the eyes brighten. The arms, crossed across that chest, relaxed a little. 'I haven't felt well. I've got very behind with things.'

43

Another of their silences lengthened. 'I could get her to put a rinse through. I go to a girl in that salon up the hill but perhaps it wasn't there when you lived here. Things change so much, you never know what shop's going to be where. I've got a bit of grey now, just in the front. Sometimes I get a rinse put through, to cover it up.'

Stephanie had the soap now and began slowly to trickle the warm water from her own cupped hand down that bent back. 'You can tell me the name of the salon,' she said, 'when you've had your bath and I'll ring for an appointment. It'll be good fun, you'll see. I can easily drive you up there to have your hair done. You always,' she said, 'had such very beautiful hair. Now just let me swish a bit of this soap over you. You just sit there and think about something nice.'

Tell me some of your thoughts. She watched the pen hover over the pad. What upsets you? Ugliness upsets me. She had been truthful with that. Ugliness, a sense of ugliness, upsets me. In what way do you think you manifest this feeling of upset? Not at all. I don't think it is apparent to anyone. It's an inward thing. I feel a sense of ugliness inwardly. What is the most ugly thing that upsets you? I upset myself. I feel very ugly. I feel that I am very ugly. He had looked at her sharply. Ugly? In what way? Well, there's this rash that won't get better for a start. I've always had this very sensitive skin. And I feel my thoughts have been ugly. My actions have been ugly. I feel I have made myself ugly because of those things. But, surely — she had watched the pen writing swiftly — not all your actions have been ugly? Not all your thoughts have been ugly? No, possibly not. That was when she had finally grown accustomed to lengthening silences. She had watched him wait for her to speak. Really, if I am to think about it as objectively as possible, only one of my thoughts was ugly. Only one of my actions was ugly. Is ugly. I don't know whether to use the present or past tense. We won't worry about that, not today. He was still writing. Another day we'll go into the use of the present or the past tense and perhaps we can discuss what we can do about it. Show me your arm, please. Yes, I see what you mean. The skin's quite red.

In the evening they watched television, a gardening programme, with the dedicated lack of interest of people who have nothing to do and are afraid of the emptiness they possess.

'Tomorrow,' said Louise, 'we might plant the dahlias, do you think? I think I've got some dahlias out the back, in the sunporch. Perhaps we could plant them if they haven't gone too withered. They'd make a nice show by Christmas — by New Year at the latest.'

And Stephanie, from a big tweed chair, on the other side of the old fireplace, said yes they certainly could plant the dahlias if they were worth planting and if Louise wanted them planted. Certainly they could do that. It would be nice for them to have flowers to pick at Christmastime, or New Year, if the blooms were a little late. Then she corrected herself, coughed a little to cover the error.

'It would be nice,' she said at last, 'for you to have flowers to pick at Christmas,' and when Louise looked at her with that faintly questioning gaze, that aura of innocence in her large, fine, grey eyes, she said, 'I won't be here then, will I? I just forgot for a moment. I'll be gone by then, won't I? You might be better soon. We'll plant the dahlias tomorrow but I think I'll have to leave you to look after them by yourself because I'll be gone. I'll have to go back.' And they both stopped there, Louise turning away from that indefatigably cheerful man doing the television gardening.

'Dig the hole for your plant or tree with these smooth, deep movements of your garden spade,' he was saying as he made stabbing movements into the soil, 'and don't forget to wash the spade thoroughly after use or, next time you go to get it out of your garden shed, it will be rusty. This is just a little tip that will make your gardening better and will ensure that your tools give you many years of fine —'

'I think I'll turn it off now.' Louise arose with surprising agility, in spite of the protecting arm across her chest. 'I think I'll go to bed now. I suddenly feel very tired. I'm sick of the gardening man.' Snip. He was gone.

The wallpaper in the stairwell had never been replaced. It must have been the latest fashion when the house was built and, with the peculiar ebbs and tides of style, it was now curiously in vogue again, its pattern of entwined branches and leaves, berries and wondrous bronze fruits forested the stairway, and they climbed up in the last of the dusk like two children lost in a thicket.

'Are you sure this isn't too early for you to go to bed?' Louise, leading the way, looked back to the middle landing where the dolls' pram had stood. 'Whatever are you doing, Stephanie?'

45

'I'm looking out at the vegetable garden. Isn't that what this stool is for?' Below, in the old garden, lay the old wagon wheel. 'Perhaps,' she said, 'we could plant the dahlias in those nice little wedges of soil inside the wheel. Someone's weeded it all.'

'I did.' Louise had reached the top stair. 'I felt really well one day so I got it ready to plant a herb garden, but I don't think I will now. I took a fancy to have some herbs growing just outside the kitchen door, but I've gone off the idea.'

Stephanie stepped down from the stool and ran up the last of the stairs, two at a time.

'If you want herbs you must have herbs,' she said, thinking how the tendrils of fine marjoram, the glossy wide leaves of basil on their strong stalks might somehow propel Louise forward into another better time. 'We can put the dahlias somewhere else. We'll do it tomorrow. We can go and buy the herb plants in the morning if you feel you'd like to. You can sit in the car and wait for me while I get the plants. No need for you to get too tired.' Then, suddenly remembering the shrilling of the telephone that morning, she said, 'You can tell that person who's going to ring that you want plants. I don't know where to go any more, but you'll know and you can tell him. Tell him we're going to get marjoram and fine basil and thyme and sage and parsley, all sorts of things.' Already she was imagining tall, exuberant plants, long established within the spokes of the old wheel, and Louise's voice, robust and confident, showing visitors the garden. *And this is where my cousin Stephanie planted all these lovely herbs for me when she looked after me once. Yes, aren't they doing well? I'm not sure how long they've been there. Two years? Three? I've just forgotten, but we put them in and they haven't looked back since.*

'So that's tomatoes tomorrow, and herbs.' Louise was standing in her bedroom door. Again there was that swift glimpse of the old hoop-back bed, the teddybear, the oak dressing table, its glass top scattered with small items that were almost replicas of the things in the bedroom next door. Crystal vases, some empty, some holding hat pins or broken necklaces of forgotten beads in colours that glimmered faintly through the cut glass. A sunhat, a pair of binoculars, a handbag lying half open, the contents spilled among the bric-à-brac on a large crystal tray with matching powder bowls. 'Goodnight, Stephanie. Sleep well. See you in the morning. If you'd just undo these buttons for me and slip my arm out of this sleeve — yes, Stephanie, just like that — I think I can manage but I'll shout if I need you.' The door closed, then opened again. 'Thank you, Stephanie. Sometime you must tell me how to make that lovely stew you cooked for our dinner.' She stepped forward. 'And I must kiss you goodnight,' she said and Stephanie felt the faint brush of lips on one cheek. 'My mother always used to kiss me goodnight. Did yours? Yes?' She stood back a little. 'I think I prefer you with longer hair,' she said. 'I know those short haircuts are very in, but I think I prefer you with that long hair you used to have.'

'Just give it time, Louise — it'll grow. Where I come from everyone has short hair.'

'Yes.' There was a sudden flurry as the bedroom door closed again. 'Goodnight.' The voice, muffled by stout wood and the thickness of the old walls, seemed to be retreating.

Seven

BASIL IS A TENDER plant with regard to season and weather, but there its tenderness ends. It is a herb of Mars, carrying with it a virulence of such strength that it will draw to it virulence from other plants and beasts. Apply a basil leaf to a poisonous wound and the poison will be drawn out, so does noxiousness draw noxiousness to itself. Basil will not grow with rue or even near it because rue is an enemy of poisons. The seed of rue, placed in wine, is an antidote to poisons.

Sage, a shrubby plant found in many gardens, has long, rough leaves. It was considered, in ancient times, to be good for the liver and to facilitate the breeding of blood. A decoction of sage leaves was supposed to expel a dead foetus, make the hair black, have a diuretic effect on those with urinary problems, clean a filthy wound and stop bleeding. This juice, drunk in warm water, was also said to help hoarseness and a cough.

She stood at the window, looking down into the darkening garden, small sounds of movement in the room next door gradually diminishing. Drawers slid gently in and out. She turned her head, listening like an intent and hunted creature that keeps an ear cocked. And she had become like that, she thought as she turned back to the window. She was like an animal that had to nose its way this way and that, listening for danger and also for ways to ensure some kind of survival, even momentarily. Food, friends, a safe place to rest, how to snatch a moment or two of impregnability. The skill to obtain these things had been laboriously learnt and was slow now to go away.

In the morning, as she surveyed the old garden again, she thought it would be best not to say what she had learnt of herbs because Louise would reply, in her incomparable innocence, 'My word, how did you know all that?' And she might be tempted to say, just naturally in that way people have when they talk easily to each other, 'I read a lot. At night there wasn't a lot to do, really, so I read a lot. One year — I can't remember when it was, perhaps it might have been two or three years ago, but it doesn't matter — I read a lot about herbs and ordinary garden plants. Did you know, for instance, that an ointment made of thyme was supposed to take away warts and swellings and dullness of sight?'

It would be better not to say anything like that because Louise would just murmur, 'Oh,' in that breathlessly innocent way she had when she knew the answer and it embarrassed her. 'Oh? Really? I must just pop up to my room and make sure I've put my keys in my purse. I've suddenly got a notion I've mislaid them.' There would be the sound of retreating footsteps, a door closing, feet on the stairs, the deathly silence of extreme perplexity.

Best not to say, 'They were quite kind, really. They gave me a copy of Culpeper's Complete Herbal one year and I used to memorise great tracts from it to keep my brain in trim. I thought it was best to harness my own mind and learn a few things rather than be depressed. The pills make you feel so blunted, so dull-witted, you know.'

Best not to mention that mint was once used as a treatment for hysteric depressions and complaints of a similar nature and that the juice from its leaves, when dropped into the ears was thought to relieve deafness and pain, though it was never much used for such a purpose. That mint juice, when mixed with vinegar, helps dandruff. That she had silently and secretly eaten mint leaves herself when she took her turn for work out in the vegetable garden between Blocks A and B. She hoped they would relieve her own sense of rising panic and horror, that she might cease to cry in her sleep. That common wild marjoram is under the dominion of the planet Mercury and cleanses the body of choler, relieving the bites of venomous beasts.

'I love to bite your fine, slim ankles,' he once said.

49

'Would it be all right,' she had asked once, 'if I picked a bunch of mint from the garden? You know how some days we have our turns at working in the garden? Well, could I, please, on the days when I work out there, pick a bunch of mint to bring back with me?' She had never used the words to my room, to my block, to my cell. Never that.

'You'll have to get a permission slip. What mint? Where?' And they had come with her to the farthest corner of the cultivated patch, where the land sloped a little but never enough to be out of sight, where the dampness gathered and there the common old mint grew lush and fine.

'This mint,' she had said, planting herself squarely beside it. 'It's just ordinary mint, like anyone puts in the saucepan when they cook new potatoes. I just want to pick a little bunch of it and take it back with me to keep in water beside my bed overnight.'

When they looked at her in that calculating way they had, she said, 'Look, it's just mint. Taste it. Smell it.' And she had torn a leaf apart. 'Here, take a piece, smell it. It's just mint.'

She had become a connoisseur of silences and when another one lengthened she had said, 'I read about mint in that herbal book you let me have. Mint taketh away the evil humours and lightens the soul. Mint —'

They stopped her, one of them with his hand raised. 'Yes, yes.' They were sick of her by then, a thin, intent woman with a bad history setting herself firmly by a ragged mint bush in an enclosed garden miles from the main road. With justification miles from the main road, and enclosed by barbed wire fences. 'I suppose you can.' One had spoken first. 'Yes, yes. I suppose that will be all right.' The doubling of the words somehow like two sharp blows. Then there had been that revealing look of sudden suspicion. 'What do you plan to put it in?'

'Just a tin mug,' she had said. 'I know I can't have a glass. I'll put it in a tin mug. If necessary I'll just put it, dry, beside my bed and breathe in the mint smell all night as I sleep and I'll throw the dead cuttings away in the morning. I mean no harm,' she had said, still planted squarely beside the mint bush. 'I mean no harm. I've had a tin mug for years. If I put some mint cuttings in it overnight I can't see that I've made the tin mug any more dangerous or any more prone to cause suspicion than it was before I wanted to put mint in it overnight. Please, let me have the mint.' It was as close to begging as she had ever come. It would have been more logical to beg on other subjects. Please, let me have the light on for longer. Please, let me have a room with a bigger window. But it was the wish to sleep within the framework of the scent of mint that finally broke her. 'Please, please,' she said, 'oh please.'

'What's this I hear about evil humours?' That was the man with the notebook. So they had noted her words, she thought.

'It was only something about mint — the garden herb, mint — that I read in that herbal book. Mint chaseth away the evil humours,' she said, 'or something like that. And hysterical depressions,' she said. 'It chaseth away the hysterical depressions.'

'Ah,' he said, 'perhaps we could talk about depression. Now, tell me honestly, do you ever feel depressed — so depressed, for instance, you feel you can't go on?'

'I did feel like that,' she said, 'just the once.' And when the silence lengthened again, she said, 'But I did something about it, even though it was probably the wrong thing and somehow, after that, I felt both more and less depressed, but in a more manageable way. But I see perfectly now that the other man who was here, the other one who used to see me, was exactly right — that there were other things I could have done which might have been more damaging and less damaging, but in different ways, and I also see I should have done it in France, if I had been able to get there. But I couldn't do that, because I didn't have the fare.' After the silence became almost solid she said, 'I'm just joking.'

'I see,' he said, and closed the notebook. 'Perhaps that might be enough for today.'

What is your opinion of this flippancy you claim the defendant exhibited during the interrogation? the constable had been asked during the trial. I found it disgusting, he said. It was difficult, as I've said, to see where the defendant was coming from. I was not being flippant. She had stood up then. I was not being flippant at all. They went on and on when there was no need to. I was tired. I was sick of it. I told them all about it. I gave them the knife. I went there myself, to the nearest police station, of my own volition. What more did they want? What more do you want? If there are any more outbursts of this kind you will be charged with contempt of court. Please resume your seat and remain silent.

'I felt quite depressed about coming home,' Louise said at dinner-time, 'but I feel better now. It's nice to hear someone else in the house. I used to sit in the hospital and worry about coming home, but I don't worry about it now because I can see everything's quite all right. But I do worry about you, Stephanie. I see your light on late at night. Whenever I wake up there's your light still on, shining out over the lilac tree. Don't you get tired?'

'I suppose I do.' She had sounded very laconic, dishing up the meal with a lazy kind of ease. It was, she thought, surprisingly simple to cook for two people when she had become accustomed to helping in a kitchen that produced meals for so many. 'But it's a luxury for me to stay up late at night, to sit reading and writing till very late with the light on.'

'Oh.' There was Louise's sudden embarrassment again. 'This is delicious. You must write the recipe out for me, so I know how to cook it when you've —' and she stopped there, the voice too sudden, too quick again. Gone, thought Stephanie. Been taken back. Been returned. 'When you aren't here any more.' Louise, rallying now, continued to eat the dinner.

Later in the evening Stephanie began to write out the recipe in a high, sharp style, the upswinging strokes that formed capitals like the movement of a knife. The old clock downstairs struck midnight, the sound of the chimes coming thinly like remnants of memory. Her reflection in the mirror of the dressing table looked like that of someone she did not know. The face so pale. The hair so sleek. Eyes so faded. Once that mirror had held the twin reflections of a mother and a little girl, both faces vivid with embarrassment. I can't bear to look. That was the mother speaking. Stand on that stool and look out the window quickly — see if it's him. Tell me if it's him. From outside they could hear sounds of shouting, of raised voices. From the stool she would recount the unfolding story of arrival — yes, it was him, her father. Yes, he had that lady with red hair with him again. He was shouting things. He was saying — Yes, yes, her mother would say. I've got ears. I can hear him.

The high windows of the upstairs bedrooms opened easily, even though they were old and the hinges were rusty in places. The paint on the frames was cracked and peeling, and must have swollen in many wet winters and dried and baked in dozens of summers, yet the windows swung out easily into the soft, dark night, the bars of light falling again over the lilac tree and on to the roof of her car, which was still parked in the same place. The day had passed swiftly and they had not gone to the tomato gardens and nor had they made space in the shed for her car. The hours from Louise's bath and Louise's dinner, when she had gently spooned out the beautiful stew on to Louise's plate, had passed quickly.

The coast was half a mile away and tonight the wind was blowing inland, bringing with it the scent of the ocean and, from far away, it was possible to hear the waves breaking. Perhaps, she thought, they could go down there, down to the sea, one day when there was time, after Louise had had her hair cut and after they had gone to buy vegetables. Tomorrow, she thought, there would be time for all that tomorrow or the next day, and she returned to the dressing table. There she had drawn up another tapestry stool, the twin of the one on the landing beneath the stairwell window but with higher legs, so she was agreeably positioned to write easily.

She had stood beside Tony in the little staff kitchen at the end of the main corridor. Have you got your apron, Stephanie? Please, put it on then. Tony, I hate wearing an apron. If you wish to be a cook, you must wear one. Now put it on, please. Don't think of it as anything but a badge of office, Stephanie, a sign of officialdom. The chef is king of the kitchen — now put on your crown. Okay, okay, she had said, keep your hair on. Always remember, Stephanie, all dishes have a secret and the secret of this one is, firstly, to prepare the meat very neatly like this. See how I cut the fat from the sides, how I trim it with this very sharp knife so the shapes are perfect little squares like matchboxes? Apart from never giving in to the temptation to put water in the bowl with the meat before you cook it, that is the great secret of this really classical cottage dish, Stephanie — the neatness of the squares of meat and the sharpness of your knife. See how the blade quickly slits the fat away from the good meat? Slit, slit, just like this? I keep it razor-sharp because it makes the preparation so much easier if you have a really sharp knife. Thank you for offering to help, but no — I think I'd better do it myself. I should, really, have brought the meat with me all trimmed up but, somehow, it just slipped my mind. Of course, he said, the knife, my knife. What slipped your mind, she had wanted to say, looking at Tony, looking at the kind little man who, suddenly, seemed more suspicious and more knowl-

edgeable than she had guessed. Did you forget just for a moment, Tony, that you weren't supposed to bring a knife here? Was that what slipped your mind, just for the tiniest second? She had wanted to say those things, but did not.

When he left that day she said, Well, goodbye Mr Bernadino, and wondered later, in her room, if he had noted and noticed her rebuff and her recoil. I usually come along the corridor with you and wave goodbye from inside the doors — from inside the grille inside the doors to be absolutely accurate — but today I've got a rather sore ankle, Mr Bernadino, so I'll just stay here if you don't mind and I'll wait for them to come and get me. Perhaps you could call into that office on the left, just past those big blue painted doors, at the top of A Block and tell who-ever's in there that I'm here waiting, will you? Thanks so much, Mr Bernadino, and she had used his full name carefully and deliberately, like a slap. What's this about an ankle? Someone she had never seen before came and collected her. Oh, it's nothing. Mr Bernadino shouldn't have mentioned it. It's probably nothing. I might have twisted it a bit when I was out working in the garden yesterday. I think it'll pass in a day or two. If it continues please report it. Perhaps we could arrange an X-ray. Thank you. How kind. We're not unkind, you know. If it's pain-ing you we can have it investigated. Thank you. I feel it might pass off in a day or two. And she had gone back to her room to look at her reflec-tion in the tiny mirror, so small it was not possible to see her whole face at once, and she noted that her wide grey eyes looked stony these days and that two faint silvery wings of paler hair had somehow appeared at her temples in the last three or four years. It really doesn't worry me, she said, when they asked her about the ankle again. I'm fine, really I am. I'd forgotten about it. Perhaps I imagined it.

Below the windows of the bedroom, the garden lay silently, dark with promise, lilacs that were purple in daylight now blooming black against an old white wall.

'I didn't realise you knew so much about plants and things.' Louise, today, had stopped suddenly in the drive. They were on a circuit of the garden. 'I thought they were just old grape hyacinths. Tell me again. Tell me what you just said again.' So she had heard her own measured voice reciting the information a second time. 'Exquisite little bulbs for the open border,' she heard herself say. 'They also make pretty pot plants for early flowering, but they should not often be disturbed. Three variations of the breed — *Muscari botryoides*, *M. b. alba* and *M. b. pallida*.' When Louise stood there silently, looking at her own garden almost as if she had had a fright, she said, 'I memorised all that from an old gardening book, an old catalogue, really. I read a lot. Sometimes there wasn't much else to do but memorise things, just for some way to pass the time. But I've said that before.'

'Yes, I'm beginning to see.' Louise, though, had seemed less embarrassed. Familiarity, even for just a couple of days, had perhaps made her feel easier with the idea of someone reading in a cell, which was always called a room but was a cell nevertheless. She did not, this time, say 'Oh,' and hurry away. 'When we go round the back of the house I must show you my mint. I'm quite proud of it. People say it's easy to grow but my plant's extremely luxuriant and it never dies back, not even in the winter when they often do. I must show you.'

Blood. The day had been a curiously hot one in mid-April that year, when earlier storms had taken the true summer away. In April, though, the nights had been sweltering, hot enough to boil her blood, and a sudden rush of huge mosquitoes, swollen with the hot blood of neighbours, flickered around the lights in her house. Are you all right? His telephone calls since Christmas had been oddly sporadic, the old routine of a daily call at exactly nine in the morning somehow changed to rushed exchanges from public callboxes, his voice oddly flummoxed so the lies were more noticeable. I'm going away sailing tomorrow, no the day after, no Friday, no Thursday. Well, make up your mind, she would say, standing on one leg like a child beside her little hand-painted telephone, pretty as a toy. Both of them, she and the telephone, pretty as toys then. I might be able to have lunch tomorrow but I'm not sure, Stephanie. I'll have to ring at the last moment. I'm not sure what she wants to do. She might be here and she might not. I'm not sure if she's going to work. She might work from home tomorrow, I don't really know. I'm not sure what my plans can be till I know what she's doing. You do understand, don't you? Oh good. Mostly he did not wait for her reply. Don't bank on me, though. No, I won't. She had been stung then. I never do. You know I never do. I know, I know. He had sounded tired. She's playing up again.

55

She gets very hysterical. They're a very highly strung family, they're all like that. It runs in the family. They're easily knocked off their perches. She has a brilliant mind, a brilliant, brilliant mind, I must say that for her. Nonsense, she would say. Rubbish. It's just that they've never been knocked back. She's never been knocked back. You can only be hysterical, you can only be a hysteric, if you've got victims to terrify. If you told her to shut up she'd stop having hysterics because it would be no use. You don't understand, Stephanie — I do love you, you know that, but I've got to look after her. She needs me. I can't divorce her, I've told you that dozens of times, because she's so ugly no one else would marry her. She'd never get another husband if I left her, so I've got to stay. You must understand that. I do.

Her voice, that April, had held a peculiar finality which he had never detected. I do understand everything. You would be very surprised what I have come to understand. I haven't really got time, myself, to have lunch tomorrow anyway. I've got to go out and work in the garden. And she would lie then, extravagantly and blatantly in a way only she could invent. I'm propagating roses, she would say. And I've got to make a rose junket. Both activities are highly specialised crafts so I really haven't got time to have lunch with you till next week, anyway. Much later she would work quietly in her sitting room in the evenings wondering if he ever noticed, at that time, that she ceased to say take care, and she would just say, coldly, goodbye.

Eight

THE OLD HOUSE stood on a slight rise, several feet above the street, the front garden and lawn boxed in by brick walls and only the tops of its trees clearly visible from the pavement outside. Through the branches of lilacs, chestnuts and oaks, the upper dormer windows jutted. The blinds were always down now, the old holland fabric giving an air of guileful withdrawal from the street and, inside, a slightly fusty atmosphere of secrecy that was restful and reassuring. At the sides of the blinds, where the fabric had curled back in the heat of many summers, it was possible to obtain slivers of views — a stripe, brightly coloured, of the chemist's shop window opposite, a slice of the sign of the butchery, one leg of a passer-by walking on the other side of the road, a broom being operated vigorously out on the pavement in front of the corner dairy, the red handle held by only one visible hand of a boy, or a flat-chested girl, in a blue jersey.

At the side of the house, small latticed windows, one for each upstairs bedroom, had been built beneath the eaves and it was possible to open these after pushing aside net curtains strung on wire, the brown blind going up with a sudden flick, again like that of a knife. The view from there was different again, the sound of traffic very faint through the trees. Below, the old lilac was stirring in a light breeze off the sea, gulls wheeling overhead in idle circles. It would rain later in the day, she thought as she leaned out, and the birds had sensed the coming of a storm.

From this very elevated side of the house it was possible to see only backyards, loitering like secrets behind houses with bland façades. As she watched, she saw a large yellow dog run towards someone unseen who was calling from round the corner of a bungalow away to her right. The dog disappeared, its glad barking echoing through the treetops. At the house next door a sullen woman came out through the door of an outside wash-house. She stood there for a moment, bare-breasted in the early morning sun. A much younger man came out of another door in the house. He kissed her passionately. They went inside. The door slammed. The dog had gone. The barking ceased.

She stood at the upper casement in her rough pyjamas, listening to the echoes of memory and spectre. Once she had had a golden dog. It had run towards her barking. Bare-breasted, she also had been kissed passionately and had then gone indoors, the resonance of the door's slam enticing and delicious.

How long had you known this man? they had asked. Quite a long time. How long? I have forgotten how long. They had conferred then, whispering to each other from their official position on the other side of the table. We are getting an impression here of concealment, perhaps wrongly. Could you please make your answers more specific. Could you phrase your answers more specifically. Okay — could I have a piece of paper and a pen, please? She did small sums down the margin. I knew him for quite a long time, she said at last, but if you want to know exactly how long I have just worked out, and checked it, that I knew him for three years, eleven months, two weeks, five days and fourteen hours. As you may recall, it was exactly at 2 p.m. on the day in question that I killed him, hence my mention of the fourteen hours. I met him for the first time at a dinner party but it was about midnight that night before I really spoke to him or found out his name because it was a largish party and I didn't really say hello to him till I was leaving. He said, I've been wondering all evening if you'd like to have lunch with me sometime, and I said, okay, it's nice to get out and about. I don't go out much, I said, or not with people. Mostly I go out by myself, I said. So I wrote my telephone number on a paper dinner napkin with his pen — it was the only paper he had — and I went home. That's how I met him. And it was about midnight. Thank you — perhaps we can take a short break now, you might like to have a rest. No, she had said, I'm fine, really, just fine. I can't see what the problem is because I've told you all about it, I've told you what I've done — what I did — so is this really necessary? Already the tenses were becoming blurred. Is it necessary? That, said the biggest one, a man with a red face, is for us to say, I think. Oh yes, of course. And she hung her head then. I had forgotten, she said. You had forgotten the incident? Oh no — she had become slightly expansive then — oh no, I could never forget that, but I meant I had forgotten — and then she had stopped. How could it be lucidly explained that she had forgotten she was not in charge of herself any more, that she was in their charge now. Nothing, she said. Nothing. Forget it.

She padded out to the landing, over the mat made from the last good piece of the old bluebell carpet, to Louise's bedroom door, slightly ajar this morning. The clock downstairs was striking eight now and there had been no dawn stirrings from Louise, no early morning tea as there had been yesterday, just silence broken by the ticking and chiming. Curled up like a child, Louise lay with one hand holding the edge of a pink blanket and the other arm guarding her chest, that hand upon her heart. But there was a slight rise and fall of those ribs, the faintest sound of an inward breath so, aware always of their rules of intrusion, she backed away and went down to the kitchen to put the kettle on. There was a legend in the family that one of the old second cousins had never even played with anyone as a child, and he had grown up in a family of six children. He had always, even when he was three years old, pinned a sheet across a corner of any room and had played alone behind its bland privacy.

She tiptoed away. Perhaps it was a good sign, she thought, that Louise had slept so well. Nine out of ten for care and nurturing. Or perhaps it was a bad sign, denoting that she had been allowed to become too weary. One out of ten. Good sign/bad sign. What did it all mean, she wondered as the water heated and the kettle began to purr slightly, like a fond cat beside her in the curiously old and curiously new kitchen. The refurbishments, she decided, had flummoxed her.

I think it's a bad sign, she had said once to one of her friends. It's a bad sign that he rings so seldom now and talks to me so briefly, that his visits are so sporadic, and brief too, and that I tell him things he never remembers. He doesn't listen. He forgot my birthday. Oh I don't know,

her friend had said, my husband's like that. Perhaps it's a good sign real-
ly. Perhaps it's a sign that you're like an old married couple, that you're
used to each other. You know? No, she said, I don't know. I don't know
anything like that, I know nothing at all.

On an old stone wall outside the windows a grey cat sat, sunning itself. The corn might have grown half an inch in the night, she thought as the telephone began to ring and from upstairs came the faint sound of a pair of feet hitting the floor. The faraway inner sounds of two-storey houses are an arcane realm of knowledge studied intimately by people who have inhabited such places. The stairs were creaking now and then there was a blurred, 'Hello,' as the receiver was lifted. It was the daily call about their activities. About her activities.

No, they had not gone to the tomato gardens yesterday after all. There had somehow not been time, no other reason. The day had just gone, inexplicably it had sped by. And she detected in Louise's voice a faint sense of pleasure about the innocent passage of time. Another day gone. One day closer, possibly, to bad news. But one day closer, perhaps, to good news. Closer to the day they would both go down to the offices of the surgeon to have the strappings, guarded so carefully in the bath yesterday, removed. Sorry, said Louise. Yes, I'm still here. I was just thinking, that's all. I was slightly away with the dicky birds. Yes, okay, they would definitely go to the gardens today, and if a time was required, okay again, make it two o'clock. And everything was fine. No, the visitor didn't evince any interest in leaving or, indeed, in going out anywhere much at all. Dinner had been expertly cooked the previous evening. Yes, by the visitor — cooked by the visitor, who else? She was planning on asking for the same again because it had been so delicious. No, she was not nervous at all and yes, they had been put away, all of them, put right away somewhere where no one would think of looking for them. Goodbye then, till tomorrow.

'Hello.' She came padding out to the kitchen, barefooted and in her nightdress. 'Nice morning,' she said, as if they had both lived in the house together for years. 'I seem to have slept in.'

'You looked very peaceful, so I left you.' Hand on the teapot, she willed the kettle to boil. Best not to ask why Louise had slept last night with her door ajar, but locked the night before. Better to be able to say something innocent and stupid. 'Would you like a cup of tea here? Or up in your bedroom?'

'I told them' — Louise's attention had been caught by the cat now — 'we'd go to those gardens today definitely. Anywhere for the tea — I don't mind. And there's that cat again.' She leaned forward, intent upon the animal which began to wash its face, perhaps sensing the pleasantries of possible later adoption and, thus, a necessity to make itself look as handsome as it could. 'I've seen it out there before in the early morning.' She presented her elliptical conversation with the confidence and knowledge that everything deleted between subjects would be instinctively understood. 'Lots of times.' They were a telegrammatic family, thought Stephanie, dealing with the smaller bones of skeletal communication. The backbone had to be divined.

'Righto,' she said in answer to all remarks, and began to slice bread for their toast.

'I didn't ever realise you knew Uncle Tom very well.' Louise was still watching the cat.

'I didn't. I hardly knew him at all. I think I saw him only from a distance, really, even in his own house, even on his own farm. I think, somehow' — and she stopped there, the hopeless bread knife suddenly still amid the crumbs — 'everyone must have fallen out over something, perhaps the grown-ups all had some row or another over something silly when I was a little girl. I don't know.' She waited. 'I'm afraid this bread's rather sawed up. This knife doesn't seem to be very sharp. I'm just going to give you a piece of toast to start off with, then I'll make porridge.'

'Oh good,' said Louise, 'and no, it isn't. It's the worst one in the house. Just do your best. It'll do.' She was still watching the cat, which had begun to stroll away along the top of the wall. 'Perhaps they did fall out. I do seem to remember something.' Her voice contained a mysterious certainty, her knowledge more specialised and more detailed because she was older and might have had the wit to eavesdrop more authoritatively at the time, thought Stephanie. They had probably all had a difference of opinion, she thought, over property of some kind, over whose farm was better than someone else's, about whose pig had won second prize at a small and distant show when it was thought to be unsuitable for such elevation as it had one lop ear and a tail that was neither pink nor curly enough, about whose daughter had married better than someone else's, about who had three bridesmaids in pink when two brides-maids in blue were all that was warranted. It could have been anything. But she recalled when the fleeting calls to afternoon teas of crackers with tomato neatly sliced on top, a drift of pepper and salt, had ended. Their abbreviations were not all conversational but often involved flesh as well.

'Breakfast,' she said, and put Louise's toast on her plate.

'It's definitely better on three, isn't it?' said Louise but, easily follow-ing the ellipsis of thought and circumstance, Stephanie knew immedi-ately that she meant the toast was not burnt as it had been yesterday. 'I hope it comes back tomorrow.' That was the cat. 'Perhaps,' she said, 'we could give it something to eat, could we? Tomorrow?'

'I don't see why not.' Stephanie had opened a large cupboard. Her voice, even in her own ears, sounded muffled by the stout walnut doors. 'I'm looking for more cups,' she said, 'but I can't seem to find any. I thought you kept china in here, didn't you? Wasn't the china cupboard always here? In this corner? I thought I remembered some breakfast cups being in here — big cups, you know the sort of thing. I thought this was where you kept the dinner sets. And all the extras.' The shelves of the cupboard, which went from floor to ceiling, stretched out, pristine and empty. There was not even an eggcup anywhere in there, not a tea strainer. 'And the tea sets,' she said. 'Weren't they always kept in this cor-ner of the kitchen? Didn't you have a pink tea set for pink moods and a green tea set for green moods and a blue tea set — blah blah blah, end-lessly on?'

'Um.' Louise, one arm crossed against the bodice of her nightdress, looked caught out, like a thief in her own house. Again, the silence lengthened. 'I just don't have all that stuff any more,' she said at last. 'It was far too much for just one person. It was all sold. I sold it.'

'But it was lovely.'

'I didn't need it, so it was all sold. I don't even think about it any more. It was ages ago. Years ago. Just rinse out a couple of those cups in the sink, they'll do. I don't bother about tea sets and dinner sets any more. I don't have any visitors. If anyone does come for a cup of tea, I just rinse out one of the kitchen cups.'

It seemed to have become a morning of delicate revelations, thought Stephanie.

'But you were always so hospitable. I remember when you used to give dances. I remember when you used to roll up the carpets in the front rooms and people used to dance.'

'I don't bother any more. I don't see people any more. I keep myself to myself.' Louise began to spread marmalade on her toast. 'It doesn't worry me, honestly it doesn't, but,' she said, peering out the window again, 'I'd really like to keep that cat if it doesn't belong to anyone else. It'd be company, wouldn't it?'

'There isn't any reason why you can't have the cat if no one else wants it. Now — would you like more toast before I make you some porridge?' Louise shook her head.

There isn't any reason, Miss Beaumont, someone had said — was it a warder, a constable, a lawyer, somebody anyway — why you cannot be paroled much earlier than the length of your sentence suggests. With remission for good behaviour and various other things that can be considered — well, I can't possibly give you an exact time for your release but, if I were you, I'd throw away the idea of the numbers bandied about today, Miss Beaumont. I'd throw them right out the window. Mrs Beaumont actually, she had said, wanting somehow to keep him quiet, to snub his kindness so she could remain rigid as a bas-relief with no inner thoughts, a carven image presented flatly and stonily to the world. May I go back to my cell now? We do always try to call them rooms. Or, if you would prefer, quarters. Yes, you may go back to your quarters now if you particularly want to. And she had liked that, the idea of having just a fraction of something. Quarters. A quarter of a life, a quarter of a marriage because her husband had died young, a quarter of a much later alliance. Not even a quarter, she thought. What fraction of a week is three hours on a Thursday when each weekday has twenty-four hours and there are seven days in each week to split the arithmetic further? Even only an hour and a half some weeks if the wife were throwing one of her tantrums, so the total could be halved again. And there were the holidays, the trips abroad on business, the family Christmases that caused lengthy absences, many weeks a year with no visits at all.

'Stephanie? Are you going to stand there forever, staring into that empty cupboard? If you must make porridge you'll find the rolled oats in the next one along — the bottom door, that's right. It looks to me as if it's regularly fed, as if it belongs to someone. The cat, Stephanie, the cat. Had you forgotten what we were talking about?'

'No.' Her voice, she thought, sounded very leaden, a heavy, dull voice belonging to a woman without animation. 'Now, how do you like it? Thinner rather than thicker? Okay.' And she stood measuring out the oatmeal into a small saucepan, adding the water, stirring it all up with exquisite precision while blackbirds pecked vigorously on the little lawn outside the windows and thrushes sang beyond the boundary fence. 'Yes,' she said, 'you're right — it does look fed.'

You could go for a walk and look at the shops down the road if you like, the man with the notebook had said once. I could arrange it for you. The regulations have changed, and I could arrange it for you. Some of them are playing golf, you know, at the local club. Just at off-peak times, of course. No, thank you. I'll just stay in here, she had said. I'm really quite happy listening to the birds singing and wondering where they've come from and where they might go. I've got a book about it. I don't think I want to go anywhere myself any more. There are plenty of places for me to walk here. And I've already told you, I quite enjoy studying the colours in the stones and in the trees and things. They differ from season to season, you know. It's not always the same. You'd think it was always the same, but it isn't. It's peculiarly different from one season to another and even one week to another, depending on the light and the weather.

'I don't think you should give up hope of it being a stray for a few more days yet.' She was dishing up the porridge now, pouring it into an old plate with a worn blue border. 'There you are, Louise, eat that. It'll do you good. And if you really want a cat, if you're really set on the idea of having a cat, we'll get you a cat from the pet shop if that one out there belongs to someone. Is there still a pet shop down near that corner in town where the big bakery is?'

'Was.' Louise was spooning up the porridge. 'This is delicious,' she said. 'There's a restaurant there now. That baker that was there, well he died and his sons sold out to some Italian who started up a restaurant. But the pet shop's still in the same place.'

'So, Louise' — Stephanie was nearly triumphant — 'we're not done for yet. If you can't have the cat out on the fence we'll go and get you another one. We could get you a kitten. They always have kittens at pet shops and, if they don't, we'll book in for one.'

Are you very close to your cousin? The man with the notebook regarded her carefully, the flecks of hazel in his eyes more marked that day. She had got into the habit of studying his eyes, of trying to sense what lay beyond that bland expression, that unshocked exterior. I've heard you say several times, Stephanie, that she's the only member of your family that you hear from. She's the only member of my family full stop, she had said. There aren't any more of us left. We're a dying race. Did he go home, she sometimes wondered, and did he say, I've had to spend an hour talking to the vile, heartless bitch who killed that stockbroker? I've told you about her. She's the one where they never found out exactly what she did for an hour and thirty-five minutes after she stabbed the poor bastard. Or did he say, I was talking to Stephanie again today. I shouldn't tell you her name, darling. It's a breach of confidentiality. And yes, I'll have a martini, thanks. To get back to Stephanie — I keep her till last because she lets me go away from that place with a better taste in my mouth somehow. She sits there as if nothing's happened and she tells me about herbs and about roses and about birds and cooking. It's shocking, really — I'm not sure if she's very mad or extremely sane. Won't have anything to do with anyone except some cousin who writes to her and sends her magazines. Won't mix at all.

Nine

'DON'T YOU WANT any breakfast, Stephanie? You're welcome to have anything you like. There are cornflakes in the cupboard or, if there's anything else you'd fancy, we can get it today when we go out.' There was that brief pause before Louise's spoon cut into the porridge, lying like flummery on the old blue-edged plate. It is a sign of a truly great chef, Tony had said, to be able to cook simple dishes extraordinarily well. Think of the boiled egg, for instance. There are legends of chefs spending twenty years fully exploiting the boiled egg with all its moods and nuances. Think of porridge. There are some who say that porridge is an art form.

'Not really.' And then, in deliberately vague explanation, she said, 'I've had to have breakfast for so long, I've had to sit there and eat it or there'd be questions asked, that it's a luxury for me not to have any, if you see what I mean,' and there was one of Louise's little breathless 'Ohs' again, the head bent quickly and deliberately over the plate.

'Perhaps' — Louise was speaking too quickly again — 'we could go out into the garden in a minute? We could see what's been happening in the night, what's grown? Perhaps we could pick some flowers? If there are any? We could go out in our dressing gowns. It's very private here. You haven't got a dressing gown? I'll lend you one then. It's simple. We'll just go upstairs in a minute and find a spare one in one of the wardrobes.'

Stephanie stood watching the cat, which was still lying on the wall, possessive and proprietorial, as if it lived there, the paws almost masterful on the stonework. Perhaps, she thought, even if the cat belonged to someone else they could entice it in sometimes for an extra dinner and Louise could love it, even slightly and momentarily, for five minutes a day.

Nine out of ten for lateral thinking, one out of ten for honesty. Stephanie, there seems to be some kind of discussion, behind closed doors if you take my drift, and it might be possible to have animals here. Smaller animals, I mean. You know the sort of thing — perhaps a cat, possibly not a dog because dogs demand quite a lot of attention and our people here wouldn't quite have that sort of time to devote. You mean, she had said, the people here are locked up at night because they're murderers and thieving bashing bastards and the dog would want a walk after dark. There had been silence then. How are you feeling, Stephanie? It's not like you to be aggressive. I'm okay. I've told you already. Sleep well, did you, last night? I slept okay. I sleep okay. But how are you really feeling, Stephanie? How did you really sleep? I'm okay. I told you. Stephanie, I can't really have any sort of dialogue with you if you're going to stonewall me like this. Okay then, so you want me to stop stonewalling. So it's like this. So yes, I like dogs, so yes, I'd like to have a dog. Yes, I like cats, so I'd like a cat. I'd love a cat, or a dog. But I can't see them letting us have anything, not even a goddamn canary or a guinea pig, so I'm just not considering any possibility of having anything and, if you want to know why, it's because I've been disappointed so many times I'm never going to be disappointed again. So you feel disappointed, do you, Stephanie? No, she had said, I feel nothing and that's the way I want it. Would you rather go back to your quarters, Stephanie, as you like to call your room, and we can continue this another day. The tissues are in the drawer on the left. Okay, yes, I'd like that. I'd like to go back to my quarters now. And stuff your tissues. Back along the corridors. Back to the quarters. A quarter of a life, a fraction of attention, a small quantity of time.

The thing, she had said once, is that I'd like to be able to spend more time with you. You know the sort of thing — I'd like to go for walks with you or just talk to you more or go to the cinema, that sort of thing. I'd like to go to the library with you and we could change our books together, just like people do, and then we could go and have a cup of coffee somewhere. I'd like you to come with me to buy groceries. His astonish-

ment, and horror, had been almost a visible thing, like the cat on the wall. Don't be ridiculous, Stephanie. I don't have time for everything I need to do let alone for luxuries like spending more time with you. Of course, I'm very fond of you. Of course, I love you, Stephanie, you know that. You make my life worth living, as I've told you many times, but what with her illness — she's very bad at the moment. I've had to ring her parents to help with the hysteria. Really Stephanie, no, and I'm surprised you asked. I'm afraid I'd have to say no. And there was the evening she had said, so silkily and smoothly that it passed as a pleasantry, I think you're wise to say you're afraid, but he was, then, already turning away. Stephanie, help me find my keys. I can't find my keys. I can't be late. She's not all that well at the moment. I mustn't be late. Do you remember the time, she had said, when you didn't wake up till nearly six in the evening. You must have been very late then. It was a long time ago, of course, but I've often wondered what happened. What happened when you didn't get home till after six o'clock? There was hell to pay — now, do I look all right? I don't smell of your perfume, do I? And I'd better put my tie on again or she'll wonder why I went out with it on and came home with it in my pocket.

'Do I look all right?' They were on their way upstairs now after the tour of the garden. Louise stopped to stare at her vague reflection in the glass door of the grandfather clock. 'I should look in the big mirror upstairs,' she said, 'but I can't bear it. And I suppose we left a bit of a mess in the kitchen, did we? Never mind. We can clean it up later. One good thing about living by ourselves —' She did not complete the sentence.

Outside the cat had strayed further on to the property to lie on a garden seat near the lilac tree. Earlier they had wandered along the old concrete paths while Louise pointed out plants with such courtesy and pride that it was like being at a party and meeting the guests.

'This is my best pink geranium and these old pinks — you can't get them now. I read in a book that they're quite rare. This tree's a bit of a problem but I'm going to have it trimmed when I've got time to think about it and I hope it might come away better then.' So they had wandered along the drive and up the steps to the front lawn, past the biggest flower bed where once there had been a gazania border, parts of it still struggling with encroaching weeds. 'One of these days,' Louise said as if it were not just a daydream, 'I'm going to have time to come out here and tidy all this up.'

And Stephanie had wandered along beside her, wearing a kimono hand-painted with pale apricot irises that Louise had found in a cupboard upstairs, and she had said, 'Oh yes,' and 'Really,' and 'What a good idea,' also as if it might all be true and as if she, too, believed that they would somehow be full of energy once more, and unbroken as well. They would be two stalwart women in a garden, winning prizes at the show for Best Dahlia, Best Rose.

Then it had been time for the bath again and the bruising was paler today, the flesh less swollen, Louise more at ease with her own innocent nakedness.

'Perhaps,' she had said as Stephanie began to rub soap on her arms, 'we'd better cancel going to the hairdresser? Do you think I really need to go? Perhaps we could leave it for another day?'

'No,' she had said, firm as a wardress, stalwart as a nurse. 'I don't think so. Not unless, of course, you don't feel well enough. But it might do you good to have your hair done. It's no trouble to drive you there, really it isn't.'

You have been granted interim parole for an unspecified period — bank on it being shorter rather than longer — so you can look after your cousin. We are, at this point in time, calling it compassionate leave, but the parole board has met and has agreed to it in principle, for the time being. Please, be as helpful as possible to your cousin. This has been arranged particularly at her request. Do not, and I stress this, do anything silly and by silly I mean — And she had interrupted then. *I know what you mean, and what makes you think I'd be silly, as you call it? I have many faults, but I've never been silly. Have you not?* said the man with the black pen and the large sheet of paper, a form of some kind or perhaps an authority for release, she had thought later. *Have you not ever been silly? I stand corrected. I was silly once, but never twice,* she had said. *Do believe me.*

So then there had been the journey to the hairdresser, across town in the car, Louise sitting up very straight in the passenger seat saying, 'Left here, right here, no you can't go down that street any more, it's just one way there now. Go on to the second on the left and turn there. Yes, Doctor Morgan's house has gone. Didn't you know he died? They've made a parking lot there now and there's going to be a supermarket built at the back, according to the paper, not that I believe everything in the paper. Now, stop where that blue sign is.' When Stephanie drew in to the kerb Louise said, 'Don't look so bewildered, Stephanie — this is the salon. This is where we have to go.'

'But wasn't it a dress shop?' Oddly stupefied by the changes in a land-scape that both exactly and inexactly matched her memory of it, she leaned forward and said, 'And wasn't there a big block of flats over there?'

'Burned down.' Louise's voice contained the satisfaction of those who live in small towns. 'And the man who owned it — you might remember him, Stephanie, he was that one who swindled lots of people in one of the first big swindles even before swindles were invented — well, he didn't get any insurance because they said he set fire to it himself and then,' said Louise, 'he jumped into the sea off Wharf Seven because that's where the deepest water's supposed to be, but he only broke his leg and they dragged him out. He's in gaol now somewhere.'

'Perhaps I might meet him sometime, then.' And there had been another of their lengthy silences while they crossed the pavement and went into the salon, the girl behind the counter thrusting out a slim, tanned arm to tweak the side of Stephanie's hair.

'I could do yours, too, if you like,' she said, and began to flick over the pages of the appointment book. 'Nothing today, sorry, but perhaps tomorrow I could fit you in at three? No? Well, do think about it. And we've got a sunlamp for people wanting a tan. You don't feel you're a bit too pale? Even for current fashions? Oh well, it was just a tiny thought. Now, come this way, Mrs —.' And there was the shock of that silence, that space Louise's very unpronounceable foreign name always made in conversations. Difficult to spell, it often appeared on envelopes as a long, jerky line, a sanctuary of scribble that became the calligraphic refuge of the truly uncertain. Mrs Silence. Mrs Scribble. And that was a shock too, because in the jitterings of Stephanie's mind between reality and recollection Louise had seemed to be just Louise. Louise the adored only child. Louise the loved. Louise the successful. 'Naughty naughty.

Our highlights have been let go, haven't they? Aren't we usually sable, with ash-blonde as a contrast? I'll just get the colour chart.' Louise had been led away like an errant child to a mirrored alcove at the back of the shop, where she could view her own reflection in triplicate.

'My cousin's rather shy,' Stephanie heard her say, the voice faint as a sigh. 'She'll just sit and wait for me. You don't mind, do you, Stephanie?'

She had threaded her way through the chairs, through the other hairdressers doing other people's hair, right up to where Stephanie was being seated, neatly slotted into a narrow chair like a book being pushed back on to a library shelf. Placed. Pinioned. Held. 'Of course not. I'll sit and read a magazine. It'll be fine, you'll see.' There was a familiarity about those words now. 'It's a funny thing,' she said as she turned away, 'I've always thought of you as Louise, just Louise.' Yet, on the envelopes of her letters she had always written Louise's full name in flowing script, because such largesse was what she deserved, then the street and town in hesitant capitals, for a different reason. But perhaps her eyes had always been on just that one name. Louise. As her eyes were on one face now, Louise's reflection in the hairdresser's mirror. *My cousin Louise, my only correspondent, my only friend. Louise.*

In the afternoon, at exactly two o'clock, they drove up to the tomato gardens, Louise guarding her hair with a chiffon scarf that they had tied loosely around her neck. The fruit lay piled in cartons under beach umbrellas outside a packing shed, and while they chose what they wanted a sullen girl waited by the till. A woman who might have been her mother came out from an inner room and stood leaning against the counter, drawing on a cigarette so lengthily and thoroughly that the smoke seemed to go down to her toes.

'Aren't you that lady,' she said, 'that lives down the road a bit? In that big house behind the fence? And is that your cousin' — she gave a nod towards Stephanie — 'that I read about in the paper?' She drew deeply on the cigarette again. Once more, for different reasons than had become usual in the last two days, the silence grew profound. 'Lucky you came now,' she said. 'Another minute or two and I'd have been closing up,' and she began to bring boxes fully inside the shed from where they had been half propped up on the concrete outside, flurrying into the till to start counting the loose change. When, thought Stephanie, had a handful of small silver coins made such an angry jingle, when did money seem suddenly so loud, so aggressive? Had the half-closing of a double door made of corrugated iron ever before seemed like a slow slap on a cheek? 'Well, Debra,' the woman drew in a breath of air that sounded like an angry gasp, 'are you going to stand there all day till you take root? Haven't you got anything to do out the back?' She watched the girl go through a swing door to an inner part of the packing shed. 'Like I said, lucky you came now. Another few minutes and we'd have been closed up.'

'But it says you're open till four on the notice at the gate.'

'We please ourselves this time of year. We close up anytime. I just said to my daughter, I think I'll close up now.'

'In that case, I'll just take a few today.' Louise's voice contained an unusual silky quality. 'And if I — if we — want any more, we can come back another day.' She slowly put six tomatoes on the counter, each one individually placed with great care like a speaker who chooses words to cause maximum effect, or maximum injury.

'Don't you usually take a case?' The woman took a step back now. 'Aren't you one of our regulars that always takes a case of the beefsteaks? For relish?'

'I am.' Having her hair done seemed to have given Louise a greater certainty, thought Stephanie. She stood, elegantly slumped and hollow-chested against the counter, one casual toe pointed in a shoe that suddenly looked piercingly smart and the chiffon scarf fluttering in a faint breeze. 'But I've changed my mind this year, and I'll just take the six, thank you.'

In the dimness of the entrance hall that morning, the dark stairs rising up through the whole height of the house that was full of secrets, Stephanie had tied that scarf around Louise's neck. Just a casual knot, Louise, just like this, and stand a bit humped up, but elegant and casual, yes just like that, and hold your head up and kind of slightly on one side. Let that arm trail across the chest just vaguely, nothing tense. Keep the muscles very loose. Now, come and look in the mirror. I don't think anyone's going to notice anything, do you?

'I must say you're looking well.' The woman was rattling around in the till trying to find change for the money Louise had proffered.

'Yes, people do say that.' The falsehood was presented with enticing innocence.

Late in the afternoon they went upstairs again, the tomatoes forgotten in the kitchen, the car still not properly parked in the garage. 'We'll attend to all that tomorrow,' Louise had said, almost out of habit now.

From their separate bedrooms they called out to each other through the wall like children. Well, that was quite a nice day, wasn't it? Yes, I quite enjoyed it, really. I'm sorry about that woman at the tomato place. Don't even think about it — you should've bought a case if you usually get that amount, I could have helped you make relish. I couldn't be bothered, and I didn't like the way she went on. Don't worry about it — try to have a little rest now, Louise. You'll feel much better at dinnertime, much less tired, if you drop off to sleep. All right, see you later. I'm very pleased with my hair. Thank you, Stephanie. *Bonne chance*, Louise.

It was nearly five o'clock when she awakened, padding out over the top landing into Louise's room. The still figure under a quilt frightened her, just for a moment, but the chest was moving up and down faintly. Still alive, she thought. Everything is all right.

It was possible to open and close the back door without a sound, pulling it shut infinitely slowly so that the tumblers in the lock clicked only faintly, a curious skill of childhood remaining within the maps of the mind.

Where's that child gone now? She could remember her mother's voice exactly. Is she up the stairs at that pram again? From outside, from the sanctuary of an old bottlebrush tree that grew then beside the garage, she would listen to the opening and closing of inner doors. Not there, not here. Where's the little devil gone now? Ah, there she is outside with her skipping rope. And the window of the old pink room would open, thrust outwards by her mother's stalwart arm, reddened from gardening or washing. How did you get out there, Stephanie? Skip, skip, skip. I just came out here by myself. Sometimes I think that child's the devil incarnate.

There was still a butcher's shop over the road and, as she approached, she noted that there had been little alteration in its façade. Once she had been a regular customer there herself, walking up the road with a basket over her arm to do the shopping when she had been someone's nice wife in that town, a young mother, a concert-goer, a member of the library, a ratepayer and a good plain cook.

'Hello, Mrs Beaumont,' said the butcher without hesitation when she entered. 'And what can I do for you today? Nice to see you again.'

'I didn't think you'd remember me.' She let the fly door slam behind her, the creaking of the hinges exactly the same as she remembered. The butcher, though, was older and heavier but his eyes were still the clear and innocent blue she recalled so well and so suddenly. 'I didn't really think the shop would be the same, or that you'd still be here. I don't know what I thought.'

'How could I forget you,' he said, 'one of my best customers? And how long is it?' His gaze was so clear, so ingenuous that she wondered if he ever read the newspaper or did his life consist of the view from his shop window and the glimpses and absences it provided?

'It must be ten years,' she said, 'since I went away, since I sold the house.' It used to be possible to see part of her house from Louise's place but she had not looked for her own chimneys or her own trees since she arrived because it would be like staring at her own liver, or her heart torn out of her chest.

'They don't buy their meat from me.' She knew immediately he meant the people who had bought the property, a careful little man with a slightly cracked voice and his wife, a bulky figure in polyester. 'Allan is not a well man,' she had said several times.

'They don't know what's good for them,' she said. 'They probably wouldn't know a decent piece of meat if they tripped over it.'

The butcher took his big knife and steel from the holder hanging from his belt and began to sharpen the blade. 'What can I do for you today, then? What about a piece of fillet? I've got a beautiful fillet of beef here. Or you used to be fond of silverside, I remember?'

'Well' — and she suddenly remembered his name — 'Peter, I think I'll leave those, just for today. All I want is a nice piece of stewing steak, enough for two ladies, and you'd better cut it up for me, please, in nice neat squares — I'll wait if you're busy — because I want to make an old-fashioned drip stew again for my cousin's dinner.'

'Cousin?'

'Over there.' She pointed to Louise's house over the road also among trees, its chimneys broad and bland, and with the closed blinds of the locked rooms like shuttered eyes.

'The lady who lives by herself?' He seemed surprised. 'I never knew you were cousins,' he said. 'Well, fancy that. You do live and learn. Now I think of it, you're a tiny bit alike.' He began to slice some blade steak from a large piece he took from the window. 'It's a better buy,' he said, 'to take it whole and cube what you want, then you can put the rest in the freezer, or whatever.'

So she told him about the knives, how there seemed to be no carving knives or any really sharp paring knives even, just nothing to cut anything with at all except a blunt old breadknife with a loose handle that was difficult to grip. She watched him nod wisely and slowly, like an uncle or a brother. Perhaps, she thought, he did read the newspapers. He was the sort of man who would kindly shout, 'Long time no see — what've you been up to then?' But he had said nothing like that. Just hello. And nice to see you again.

'I'll do it for you,' he said. 'No trouble. There you are then,' and with a quick flick of his wrists, he wrapped and tied the parcel almost in the same movement, placing it on the counter with the air of a conjuror. 'See you tomorrow perhaps,' he said and went out the back whistling. 'Nice to have you back,' he called and she went away, out into the street, over the road to Louise's house again, wondering if he ever read the newspapers. JURY OUT IN MACABRE LOVE TRIANGLE DEATH. STOCKBROKER LAY IN SEA OF BLOOD.

The fact remains, she had said once, that you've had a beautiful house built for her, even though you say you don't love her and you married her only because she chased you endlessly. He always interrupted her there. You've got no idea what it was like. The endless telephone calls, the arrivals on my doorstep late at night, the pounding on my door, the screaming tantrums. She tried to kill herself twice. No, she didn't. If she really wanted to kill herself she'd have taken the pills when you left, not when you returned. If she waited till she heard your car before taking a handful — and was it really a handful or only one or two? — she just wanted to frighten you. She didn't want to kill herself at all. I know that, you know that, every dog in the goddamn street knows that. I don't know how you can be so hard, Stephanie. If I hadn't married her, no one else would have — she's far too ugly to attract anyone. She'd never get another husband if I left her. But you've still built her a beautiful house, as if she's a lovely woman whom you love. It's really for me. I need somewhere to live. She just happens to live there, too. It was endless. It went round and round in circles. It was a game. How could she hear your car in the drive when you came home unless she was already in your flat? There was that inconvenient question as well. How could she be in your flat to take an overdose of pills in your bathroom, ready for you to find the moment you came home, unless you had already let her in or she had a key to be there, possibly habitually? Don't answer. It's just a rhetorical question. I know the answer myself perfectly well. It was a game. In the end she played it in the same kind of mood you might be in when you try to look down a plaster cast placed on your broken tibia or still press a virulent bruise out of habit to see if it hurts as much as yesterday, even though the area has healed and there is no sensation of pain any more. In the end she was accustomed to having only an hour or two of company a week. In the end anything else would have seemed too much, too rich, too crowded, too flamboyant, far more than her social skills could ever manage. If he had left his wife she might have killed herself out of horror about so much company.

Why did you do it? they said the first night she was at the police station. Because I was fed up. Because I was sick of being left out of everything and I wanted to be left out permanently. A desire to kill him just came over me. Is that all you've got to say? Yes. Would you like to take a break now? Could we get you a cup of coffee or tea? No, thank you. I just want to be peaceful and quiet. I'm not thirsty.

I watched him out of sight the last time I saw him. The second to last time I saw him, I should say. The last time I saw him I also watched him out of sight, but differently.

I watched him drive away and I raised my hand to wave goodbye. I did wave goodbye, but he did not wave back at me. He never looked back at me, not once, he never for a moment looked back to see if I might be standing out on the verandah to send a last happy greeting to him, an arm raised in salute beneath the roses that grew up the posts of the old porch. There was nothing from him at all.

He walked diagonally over the road towards his car and I saw him straighten his shoulders and flex the muscles a little as if he might have believed he was casting something off. Thus freed, he set off. He had parked a short distance down the street. Always outside a different house, always down the street some distance or another. But, for an analytical observer, always on the same side of the road and always facing the same way, which might mean that the destination after the visit was always the same and the location of the visit was also identical.

He climbed in the car and stopped for a moment. I watched him reading something, perhaps some mail. Something white fluttered in his hand. He seemed to be ripping something, perhaps an envelope, then he sat there reading a letter or an account. I was too far away to see properly. He sat there reading his mail like a man starting a day, starting another day, which, again I supposed, he probably was. He had had his time with me and now he was going home to his wife, to that other life I had never viewed but had heard all about. The bookcases. The paintings. The custom-made kitchen. The mahogany staircase. The three bathrooms. The art collection. The granite benches. The walk-in pantries. Everything. And he never waved to me. He never saw me waving. He never looked back at me, not once. Is that all you've got to say? they said. Yes.

Ten

WE GO UPSTAIRS to bed at night very early, sometimes before the sun has properly set, certainly long before darkness falls. And she always says the same thing as we get to the top of the stairs. 'Now, don't stay up too late reading or writing or whatever it is you do. I see your light shining out over the trees, Stephanie, whenever I wake up. I woke up at two o'clock this morning and there you were, still with your light on.' I say, 'Hmm. Yes, you're right. It would've been two. It could even have been nearly three.' Unrepentant to the last. *Are you sorry? they said. Yes, I said, and no. Why do you say that? Because he wasn't worth it.*

I see our shadows on the wall and the sight reminds me of when I used to go up and down those stairs with my mother, when I was a little girl, but my hand is not linked with Louise's. We go up the stairs separately, two women climbing slowly and both of them at that curious age when no one looks at them properly any more, at an age when women become invisible and are not noted. There is no shadowy blemish of joined hands now on the old hand-painted wallpaper with its faded fruits and flowers, and the seagrass dolls' pram and the toys I wanted so badly have gone.

'Goodnight, Stephanie.' We always stop at the top of the stairs and her cheek brushes mine with the faintest of caresses. 'Thank you for coming to look after me.' It is a compliment, really, and I take it as one because I would have come to look after her even if I had had a choice and had been free.

I always watch her out of sight. Sometimes she goes straight into her room and closes the door. All I see then is a flash of pink — that is her bedspread — the teddybear askew on the dressing table, always the handbag somewhere, mostly open, sometimes with the contents spilled, the pillows still dented with the mark of her head after the afternoon siesta. *Make sure she rests as much as possible. Apart from that, there's really nothing you can do except see that she eats regularly.* That is what they told me, and I have done my best.

'Time for your rest,' I say every afternoon, and we go upstairs to our rooms.

'I'll have a rest if you have a rest.' She always had a very strong will.

'Okay,' I say. 'I'll have a rest too, just to please you.' I fall into a deep dreamless sleep because I am tired from my restless nights, the days filled with chores like making the porridge, clearing away the dishes, talking to her and trying to keep her mind on cheerful subjects. And all the time we are surrounded by these silent mysteries. Why are the two bedrooms on the other side of the upstairs landing kept securely locked at all times? Why is the door to the big sitting room downstairs similarly locked? Why does she make no move to go and sit in a little parlour that used to lead off the kitchen and the scullery? Her father used to sit there, in his leather chair beside the fireplace, and he would read novels with red linen covers. 'And who might this pretty little girl be?' he would ask suddenly in the gloom of the panelling and the dark leather armchairs. 'Do you think,' he would ask as if someone else might be present, 'that she might like a sweet?' And he would extend one arm slowly to offer me my choice from his box of chocolates. I might have been a wild and rare creature that could easily be frightened away. From the kitchen at the back of the house the faint hubbub would have already begun. Stephanie's given us the slip again. Where's that child gone to now? If she's gone up the stairs, after that dolls' pram, there's going to be trouble. If I've told her once I've told her a hundred times it's not hers to play with.

Why is that room, where once my uncle sat so much at ease with his books, unused and locked? Why, when once the rings they wore, the bracelets they possessed were a legend in the family, is there nothing on the dressing tables but empty velvet boxes containing only the hollows where jewellery once lay, dusty crystal powder bowls holding broken strings of artificial pearls, a little child's thin silver bangle with enamelled leaves the most precious thing I can find during my desultory midnight rearrangements in my room. It might be worth a few dollars on a lucky day, depending on the market for such things. Louise's hands are unadorned now except for a thin old wedding ring that has bitten into her flesh, the only sign that she was once married. I have a similar one of my own but it was taken off a long time ago. And the house, as well as being mostly locked and shuttered, is peculiarly silent even when we turn the radio on, or the television, because we are the only ones here, the only ones left. Everyone else has died. They died of the usual things — old age after good and useful loving lives, the odd tragic illness, an accident or two — but they still died and the only ones left are Louise and me. We are the last. When we listen to the radio or turn the television on the sound seems to fight with the impenetrable silence of the house, of the whole property, and it loses. It is like lighting a candle in a forest on the darkest night and, with its light, trying to see as far as where the trees begin to thin and brushland begins. The impenetrable darkness only emphasises the smallness of the flame.

'What did you do over Christmas?' he used to say some years, and I would say, 'Oh it was kind of quiet around here. I didn't do anything much, really.'

'You lucky thing. You don't know how lucky you are. We had visitors every day. You couldn't get a moment to yourself. I thought I'd go mad. Sorry I haven't been able to come to see you sooner but we had people to stay and then we went away for a few days to see some of the family and then she was home from work on holiday and I couldn't get away.' More silence. I am an expert at silence. 'I mean I,' he would say at last. 'I mean I had to go away. I had people to stay. She doesn't do a lot, you know. She's ill.'

And there's always somebody who loves to prattle to you about where they've gone and what they've seen. I saw that friend of yours, Stephanie, that one I've seen you having lunch with. I saw him over Christmas in a restaurant. There was a big table of them all, I suppose it was the whole family, was it? They'd booked a whole alcove, I'd say. You don't get those whole alcoves to yourself unless you've booked. They all looked very happy. There was a lot of laughter. He was sitting at the head of the table beaming. The wife's really quite pretty. I thought you told me she was awful. They all looked so happy. Mother said it was lovely to see a whole family out like that, all happy and laughing and having a good time. And what did you do over Christmas? Nothing much? It's your own fault, you know Stephanie, if you're lonely — you ought to get out and meet people. You ought to go out like your friend does, and have a good time. That's what you should do.

When he telephoned again he used to say, 'Is it that long? Surely it's not five weeks since I last saw you, Stephanie. You must be mistaken. Just let me count up. There was Christmas and then there was New Year and then I had to go away on holiday for a few days and then — yes, Stephanie, how amazing. You're quite right. It's five weeks since I last saw you. It seems like only yesterday.'

I remember once I went out and stood in the street outside my house. You ought to get out and meet people. I thought of that. I thought of what people used to say to me. Get out, Stephanie, and meet people. The trouble with you, Stephanie, is that you're too inward, you're too shy. One day, one Christmas, I had waited for the telephone to ring. Sometimes, during that day, I stood beside it, I stared at it and I willed it to ring. *Ring, ring.* The silence seemed enduring.

That year the neighbours were all away on holiday, the year I tried to make the telephone ring. *Ring, ring. For God's sake ring.* The silence seemed oppressive. No distant voices, no far-off laughter, no sound of the creaking door of the greenhouse next door being opened and closed as the old gardener went in and out tending his plants. Nothing. There was just nothing. I went out and stood in the street because I suddenly thought I might go mad in there, in my house by myself waiting for the telephone to ring. I stood out in the street and I thought if anyone went by, which they did not, I would say, 'Hello.' And they might reply, 'Isn't it a lovely day? I do like that pink rose you've got hanging over your porch like that. It's a real picture.' Perhaps people walking along the street might talk like that.

'Oh that,' I would say, 'I've taken cuttings of that rose for years and I've grown it everywhere I've lived for a long time. It's my favourite. I've never known its name, but it's really nice, isn't it? If you could wait a moment I'll run inside for the scissors and I could pick you a bunch. Of course it's not too much trouble — it's Christmas.' Then, after giving away a posy of flowers, I would go inside again, content that I had spoken to someone, even a stranger walking up, or down, the road. But no one walked along the road that day, nobody rang.

'Had a good time?' he would say. 'Went out and about, did you? Enjoyed yourself? Oh fine. Good. I'm glad you weren't lonely. I thought of you a lot, of course, but there wasn't much opportunity to ring with everybody around.' There would be a pause. 'I did get you a present, didn't I?'

I forget what age I was when I last stayed in this house. I was older than a child, but not yet a grown-up. I was just a girl. I used to hear them calling out to me, 'Where is that girl now? What has happened to that girl? It's the girl's turn to do her washing. She can have the tub now.' But that was unusual. Mostly I had done my washing long before any of them woke up.

I slept in one of the southern bedrooms upstairs, the ones that looked inland and where you could not hear the sound of the waves at night. The bedrooms that looked towards the sea were larger and better. They were called the big bedrooms. I sleep in one of them now, the front one that was always considered the very best. The bedrooms on the other side of the top landing were called the small bedrooms. They are both locked now. Mine, then, was one of the small ones and was at the back. It had a high small window, not much larger than a fanlight, above my bed and I used to stand up on the mattress to look out at the back garden. It was an idle inconsequential way to spend a moment.

The small bedrooms had their own narrow hallway, very dark and where the hand-painted wallpaper had never faded, not even now, all these years later. There was little natural light there. This hall led off the main landing where the sun shone beautifully through the stairwell window and where there was a view through the banisters to the entrance hall below. The sudden darkness of the little hall, even in full daylight, was always a slight shock. You could almost trip over the mat on the bare boards if you did not stand for a moment and let your eyes grow accustomed to the loss of light. The floral carpet with the roses and bluebells stopped abruptly where the hall began.

There were a lot of comings and goings at the house then. The telephone rang. People knocked at the door. The family owned a beach house and a farm a few miles away and people used to call on business about that property, about the purchase of stock, about beef cattle to winter over, about the water supply, about all sorts of things. About horses and about saddles and about where they were going dancing on Saturday night after the races and about who had married whom or should have and about who had kissed someone else's wife and should not have. The little sitting room downstairs, the one with the leather chairs, was always full of hastily folded newspapers still warm from hands that were now clutching the steering wheel of a car to back down the drive on urgent business somewhere. Farms, kissing, wives, races, horses, cattle, newspapers, stock prices, everything. It all went on there. And I was just a girl in the middle of it.

The back garden I used to look at from my bed was quite different then. There was a gaggle of hen-houses in one corner. An outside wash-house loitered crookedly under a massive grapevine and may even have been propped up by it. On Sunday mornings I used to go out there very early while everyone else was sleeping after the dancing and kissing, and I would do my washing in the big stone tub. Nobody ever danced with me or kissed me, so I was quite fresh in the early morning while they still slept. Later in the day the others would do their washing too, sometimes not pegging out their petticoats and their sheets and all the other things till twilight. Sunday was the day when the washing was done. I don't know why. Perhaps it was the only day in the week that was not filled up with other things. Other people had washing machines but we, somehow, still did all the washing by hand, with old-fashioned yellow soap. I can give no reason for this. They had many things that other people did not have — like farms and fur coats and newspapers purchased from all the main cities and magazines and trips on yachts and rings and parties and horses and kisses and dancing and large cars — but there was never a washing machine. I suppose, now, that they were all too busy to ever think of such a dull thing.

At that stage the old seagrass dolls' pram still sat on the middle landing, but I was too old for toys then and I cannot remember doing anything but glance at it as I passed by on my way up to my room under the eaves. Sometimes, on a Saturday, they would roll up the carpet in the other sitting room, the best room, and people would dance. I remember I was very shy and I would sit at the pianola. I would make the music for them all to dance to. And who did the dancing, I wonder now? I remember my cousin swinging by in the arms of a fresh-faced, fair-headed man who had something to do with horses. Did he sell them some of his horses? Were they buying a choice horse of his? I can't recall it properly. He had bright blue eyes and he never brought his wife with him. They used to remark on that. The man who never took his wife out. That is what they called him. He would stay till last of all, long after the supper trolley was wheeled in and then wheeled out again empty and long after I stopped playing the pianola and went upstairs, past the dusty dolls' pram, to my room along the little hallway.

Once he asked me to dance but I put my head down and pumped the pedals of the pianola even harder than usual and said, 'No, no, I never dance.' He looked at me rather sharply, I think. Perhaps he never asked me to dance ever again. I cannot recall ever dancing there and if anyone had asked me why, which they did not, I would have said I felt too plain, somehow unspeakable, so ugly, so gauche that it would be remarked upon. Perhaps my ugliness would be so marked, so dreadful, that I might even make the house fall down. I possess, now, an incomparable sadness about all that, about those years. The odd photograph I have seen of myself at that time shows a thin girl, slightly pretty perhaps, though the pictures are blurred as if the person holding the camera might have been dazed by dancing or horses or kissing or all three. There is nothing about how I looked at that time that should have made me think myself so ugly that I must hide. Yet that is what I thought. As soon as I had finished playing the pianola for them I would go up to my room. I thought of myself as being somehow apart, not a member of the party.

And always, as I went upstairs, I remembered the much earlier roped shadows on the wall, my mother's hand clutching mine and her urgent instructions. Be a good girl. Don't go up the stairs. Just stay in the kitchen. The toys aren't yours. You mustn't touch. And when we left, the two of us, I would have a pound note in my hand that my uncle had given me. *And who's this pretty little girl? I think a pound note might jump out of my pocket into her hand, don't you?* My mother might have things they had given her as well. I remember suede and patent leather shoes of an unsuitably fancy design that she wore when she rode her bicycle. I remember a dusky pink tweed two-piece suit that she later always called her costume. I might wear my costume, she used to say reflectively sometimes if we had been invited to a family wedding. But sometime or another, the invitations ceased, we disappeared from festivities, we were no longer seen about.

My father never came on these visits, though he was invisibly there, like the scent of smoke or the smell of dynamite. They always called him he, never his name, always just he. He had been playing up again. He had been drinking again. He had ceased to pay the housekeeping money every week. He stayed out all night. He had a girlfriend who had red hair and was called Mrs Something. Was it Mrs Elliott? Mrs Bradley? I cannot remember. He had been seen at the races, sitting in the members' stand, with Mrs Something, who was no spring chicken and was wearing a squirrel coat, full length and new. He had been very busy doing a lot of things. When I appeared suddenly in the kitchen doorway to hear snatches of all this, after my forays out into the back garden to play, the talk would abruptly cease and my mother would say, with an air of false brightness, 'Little pitchers have big ears. I must look in the oven to see how that fruit sponge is coming along.'

'Why is your face red?' I sometimes used to ask her. 'Why have you got a cold? You didn't have one this morning.' And she would say, 'I've been cutting up onions. I've been bending over the oven.' From upstairs, far away, I could hear the drumming of feet on the carpets, the hasty opening and closing of wardrobes, the slamming of drawers and my aunt and cousin would come thundering down the stairs again with things stuffed under their arms, the footsteps hasty, the packing perfunctory. A warm winter coat for you, Margaret. My mother was called Margaret. And here's a pillbox hat to wear with that pink suit. What about a nice pair of English brogues. Would you wear brogues, Margaret? You would? Oh there's a good girl, they would say to her as if she were a child too. Just try them on for size. And would this little red hat suit Stephanie? It wouldn't be too old, would it? Could she wear it to Sunday school, do you think? Would it match her coat? And how would you like some nice warm stockings, just gone a little bit in the toes — the tiniest stitch would fix them in a moment? They would peer at me, flinty-eyed I thought then, but I wonder now if all their eyes were narrowed with horror and concern. Whatever would happen to us next? I think now, too, there was something deeper, something more portentous, in their familiar question, about what I would do when I grew up.

I think it is interesting and significant that no one asked me what I wanted to do. It was not an unkind omission. Perhaps they could all see clearly that there would not be a lot of opportunities available to me, that I would not have much of a choice.

My mother's wedding photograph in their big album showed her in a long lace dress of Grecian style, holding a sheaf of lilies and smiling brilliantly at the camera. Some year or another, I cannot remember when, someone got at it with the scissors and neatly chopped the groom off. You see, I have it too, the facility for possession and the equal ability to reject.

I remember, I remember.

Eleven

DURING THE AFTERNOON of the following day they went down to the sea, skimming through the houses at the bottom of the road, through the outskirts of the shopping area, the car like a dark shark.

There had been the usual muffled telephone conversation early that morning, half heard through the gloom of the hallway and, when Stephanie had looked out through the kitchen door, Louise was sitting at the foot of the stairs, on the final and widest step, like a child unable to decide whether to go up or down. A little brass chair with a velvet seat had always been placed by the shelf that held the telephone, yet Louise had chosen to sit on the stairs as she had done years ago, when the enticements of the dolls' pram lay on the middle landing, looming above them all like a crown.

Yes, everything was going along well. The measured voice cut through the faint sound the wooden spoon made as Stephanie stirred Louise's porridge. Yes, they seemed to have slept well. It was all very quiet. Today they might go down to the coast, to the sea. What for? Nothing, really. She just had a yen to walk along beside the sea. Yes, even though it was too cold to swim yet. They still — and she made it plural this time — had this yen to go down to the sea. No, they wouldn't be going shopping because Stephanie had bought anything they needed for a day or so when she went over the road to the shops yesterday and no, she wasn't frightened. Money? Well, she had given Stephanie the purse to get the meat and things and then Stephanie had brought it back and had given it to her, yes. And, yes, she had given her the dockets, and yes, it all tallied. Everything was very quiet. Goodbye. The voice became cold and reedy then, a snub that would be incomprehensible to anyone else. Would it really be necessary to talk to them tomorrow? Perhaps they could ring the day after tomorrow as things were so quiet. Might that be a good idea? It wouldn't. All right then, tomorrow it is. Goodbye. The final word was as eloquent as the snap of the receiver back on to its cradle.

'I think you slept better last night.' Louise had come back into the kitchen now, filtering through the doorway almost like a visitor in her own house, slightly apologetic. Behind her lay the locked dark door to the little sitting room where once the chocolate box had been proffered so gently, where a pound note sometimes slipped into a small hand.

Tell your mother, Stephanie, that I want you both to go into town and buy something nice, something you might need, and here's something extra — the flush of a ten shilling note would crush into her hand — to get a nice afternoon tea for the two of you. Just tell her quietly, Stephanie, when you get home, when there's no one else about. It can be our little secret, you and me. Don't let him know you've got it, now will you, there's a good girl. But he could always smell money, her father. Had a nose for money. I'll toss you for it, Steph — double or quits. It was difficult to know exactly what that phrase meant — double or quits. Heads I win, tails you lose, okay? He would say that, a big man flushed from a day out somewhere, always with a ready smile, a canary yellow waistcoat and cold eyes. Are you ready? Are you watching? Okay, off we go. There you are Stephanie — heads, so I win. Now give me what you've got in your pocket. Give it to me, Stephanie. Fair's fair, if you won't give it to me I'll have to take it off you.

'I woke up just after midnight by my clock and your light was off. I looked out my window over the trees and there was no sign of light from your room. I think,' said Louise, 'that you're sleeping better.' Calmly satisfied and almost benign, she began to eat the porridge. 'Mother,' she said, 'always made porridge for me.' So they both sat there, in the sunny kitchen, like old children, somehow resisting the marks and the passions of the years. It seemed suitable and inevitable after that to climb in the car, leaving the dishes in the sink, and to skim lightly down through the town to the beach like girls on holiday and, once there, to breast the top of the sand dunes with a sort of ancient triumph as they had done when they were children. They even made some pretence of sliding down the other side, Louise's good arm clutched carefully in Stephanie's two hands, the slidings small and manageable so that if they tripped the little strappings across Louise's chest and up under the other arm would not tear away from that sliced and shrinking flesh. Behind them the car sat amid burgeoning tussock and sea grasses in a parking area that might not have been mowed all winter and all about them was the sound of the sea and the gulls and the waves breaking upon that untouched and deserted shore.

'Let's walk as far as the house.' That was Louise, already setting off along the sands towards where the old beach house had been, nestled behind the first row of dunes, only its red roof showing then above the rank growth of the shore. 'It mightn't even be there any more. Hurry up, Stephanie, let's go and see. What do you think it might be like?'

In the evenings they had sometimes sat and looked at one of the old photograph albums, the pictures often faded to sepia on the black pages, the writing beneath each view, each face, done in silver ink, like the wandering trail of snails. The old beach house, hidden in the dunes, had had a row of wide windows along the front, jutting like teeth on to a rough rolling lawn and, in front of this architectural grin, in various poses, they had all appeared like people in a play. All slightly self-conscious, those who were better-dressed and might perhaps have done better for themselves pert and slightly aloof, the invisible lines between cousins who married well and those who did not marked by the pointed toe of a silently eloquent Spanish espadrille of the more expensive sort, the turn of a ringed hand. Her mother had always been at the back, if she were there at all, and wore a frazzled air, her hair slightly untidy and falling down in wisps from a bun at the nape of her neck, her expression fraught as if there might be, at that very moment, something burning inside the cottage, in the little kitchen. She wore no rings at all.

Your mother was a very pretty girl, Stephanie. When she was young, people used to turn to look at her in the street. Now I want you to take her into town one day, perhaps when you're on holiday from school, and

I want you to get a really nice lunch for the two of you. There would be the familiar feel of a pound note in her hand.

The sparse population of children — they were not great breeders — hung about on the edges, scowled from behind bushes made ragged by the sea wind or lolled, plump and satisfied with themselves, in the very front row. These were the offspring of cousins who had married well and they wore swimming togs with exclusive labels and had gold fillings in their teeth, their mothers loitering with beach towels slung over slim, handsome shoulders, the hands brilliant with rings. They liked things, liked to display their things to each other, particularly if what they had might be larger and better.

'Show them your new ring, Elizabeth.' That was the dry voice of some husband or another, and the hand would be outstretched for admiration. 'It's a Brazilian diamond, that's why it's so yellow. And the other ring's a sapphire — well, a sapphire in the middle with diamonds all around. I always think it's nice to have a really large cluster, don't you. Children, don't push and shove like that to see your auntie's hand. You can all have a turn to see in due course. She might even, if you're very good girls, let you have a little try-on, just for a moment. Who wants to have first turn? Hands up for first. You must be very, very careful because it's very valuable and your auntie might cry all day if you lost it.'

There would be a pause then, time enough for someone to notice their withdrawal. 'Margaret? Where are you off to? Have you seen Elizabeth's new ring? And what did you get for Christmas, my dear? Doesn't the little girl want a turn too? No?' Embarrassment turned them into two hangers-on. They would hurry away to the kitchen, to hide their lack of gifts, their absence of ornamentation, her mother's hand gentler now and hot with embarrassment or the summer heat or distress, or all three. No one ever asked why they came alone, just the two of them with no father, no husband, no rings, no new dresses to show off, requiring a ride in someone else's car because no one drove them himself. Sometime or another he got two names. He was called he and no one. *Margaret and Stephanie have got no one. Did he come with them? No? So they had no one again, did they?*

'I must see to the scones,' her mother would call over one shoulder. 'I must just put the kettle on. I must put the salad in the refrigerator. I must whip the cream.' So they would escape from the tangible displays of affection, respect and status to sit by themselves in the kitchen for a moment or two, till lunchtime, till after the box Brownie was taken out for the holiday snaps in which neither of them wished to appear, the shabbiness eternally caught by the camera, their isolation held forever in the albums. *Margaret and her little girl Stephanie — he wasn't there, of course. He never is. They say he's even taken her engagement ring away and sold it.*

'I found this for you.' Her mother would fish around in her apron pocket to find a battered treat — perhaps one chocolate biscuit only slightly chipped and not entirely unfresh, or a segment of orange, a little sandwich made of hundreds and thousands, or sugar, anything that no one else had noticed. 'It was the last one,' she would say. 'I saved it for you. Just sit quietly on the step and eat it — don't let the others see. Let them have their rings. See if we care.' Sometimes it might be the last uneven wedge of cream sponge, the jam bleeding slightly into the cake. 'Eat it up quickly, dear, before the others see.'

Today I teach you how to make sponge. I teach you how to make Victoria Sponge, very special. But, Tony, I don't really want to know how to make a sponge cake. What use would I have for a sponge cake? Here? You'd be better off teaching me how to make a mutton pie. So, you want to learn a good way to make mutton pie, next week we learn mutton pie. This week, Victoria Sponge. Now take a nice piece of butter, like so. Please pay attention and I don't want to see faces pulled like that, thank you Stephanie. Today we do Victoria Sponge. Think of it like this — it's a way of passing the day. What other way would you pass the day? Exactly, so we make Victoria Sponge, Stephanie. In the evening, when she went along the corridor to see the man with the notebook, he said, How many marks would you give yourself for today, Stephanie? None? Why none? Because I was rude to Tony, she had said. I was rude to him about his cake and it wasn't his fault. I was offhand. I was rude in my own way, which is not the same way other people are rude, but I was still rude by my standards. I might as well learn to make a nice sponge cake as do anything else. And he had looked at her for a long time. The difficulty with you is that you won't mix, he said. They're just

91

trying to occupy you, to give you some reason to — and he stopped there. To live? To breathe? To show some interest? To stop lying on the bed with your face turned to the wall and your eyes shut? To refuse to speak or eat? But he had stopped before he said any of that. I know, and I'm sorry, she said. He's a kind man. I know he comes all the way out here from town just as a sort of thing he does to help. And it's not just me, you know, it's some of the others as well, I suppose. I think he'd like other people to go, other people to be interested in his cooking lessons. It's not just me that's a pain in the arse, it's the others as well. If some of the others would come to the lessons he'd be happier, even just one person. Ah, he said, the man who always wrote gently in the notebook, there's just a slight problem with that and I know it's ridiculous and you know it's ridiculous.

They're frightened of me, she had said. I know that. I know they're frightened of me. I'm the only one here — and again she stopped — the only one here who stabbed someone. She stopped once more. There was that woman who shot a man but it was kind of an accident. She didn't mean to do it. I seem worse somehow, carving someone up. Quite so, he said. I know that. You know that. What should we do about it? he had said and seemed genuinely puzzled, had stopped writing and sat there with the pen in his idle hand. Nothing, she said. That's why I've given myself none out of ten for today and also overall. I've given myself none out of ten forever in a universal kind of way as well. And as for what can be done about it. Nothing. I can't do anything. You can't do anything. She almost felt as if she should snatch the notebook and write in it herself, about him. He is a kind man and does his best, but some of the cases are hopeless, all written in a firm, strong, official hand like that of a doctor. All I can suggest, she had said, is that next week when Tony comes here you let me into the kitchen early and I'll make him a Victoria Sponge as a surprise so he can see I really was listening and I did kind of learn how to do it even if today was a disaster, and then he can teach me the mutton pie he mentioned and everything'll be all right again. Is there anything else you've got to say? he said. I haven't heard you talk so fluently for a long time. I dunno, she said, just give me a minute or two and I might think of something. Only joking. I might go back to my room now, thanks.

'Tonight,' she said, as they breasted the last dune, 'I'm definitely going to make you a Victoria sponge for your dessert. It wouldn't take long, half an hour at the most. You've got butter in the refrigerator, haven't you? And eggs and sugar and stuff? Okay then, it's a bargain.'

'Whatever made you think of that?' Louise was regarding the old cottage with care. 'The windows are all different,' she said. Behind them the beach stretched back to the carpark, their footsteps still clearly marked on the damp sand. 'They've taken out those old windows that went all along the front, those ones with the little panes, and they've put in those doors. I'm not sure I like it.' She stood with her head slightly tilted, as if she might be contemplating buying the place. The old gypsy look of crooked chimneys was gone and had been replaced by the straight finger of a gas flue. 'Did you ever come here? I can't remember seeing you. Are you in any of the photos?'

'I was usually in the kitchen. I must just be in the back of some of the pictures, kind of peeping round the corner or something like that.'

'Why were you usually in the kitchen?'

'I don't know,' she said. Another lie.

Have you been skiing? The cousins who had gold in their teeth specialised in expensive questions. Do you have tennis lessons? What school do you go to? Where is it? I've never heard of it. Where did you get that dress? I've never seen a funny dress like that before. Is it home-made? Why is the hem like that? My mother bought my dress. All my dresses are bought. Can you swim? We can all do breaststroke — we have lessons every Tuesday and we have French lessons on Wednesdays. Parlez-vous français, mademoiselle? Vous n'êtes pas très belle, *ha ha. If you want a job you could top and tail those beans for me, her mother would say when she slipped into the kitchen. Don't you want to play with the others? They're all out there having a lovely time. Why don't you want to go and play? You're an odd child, aren't you? Fancy wanting to be hidden away in this funny old kitchen with me when you could be outside playing lovely games with the others.*

'I've got a lot of photographs back home of those old summers. I must get more of them out tonight and have a look.' Louise was turning away

93

now, looking back towards the car. 'Did we walk that far? But the time seemed to go so quickly, Stephanie.'

'It's not so very far.' She was taking Louise's arm now, leading her down from the sandhills, to the flat beach again, where their footprints showed them the way back past the rock pools. The cousins in new togs every summer found sea anemones and shells undamaged by the tide there.

Look what Henry's found. Isn't he a clever boy? It's such a pretty shell, Henry. It looks most unusual, as if it could be in a museum. Aren't you clever? If Stephanie wasn't so silly and would go out and play with you other children she might find something nice, too, mightn't she?

'I think we'd better go, Louise. When we get home I want to make you that Victoria Sponge for your dessert,' she said, enticing Louise forward with the idea of a treat as if she might truly be a child again, 'and it takes at least half an hour to get the mixture in the oven and that's not counting cooking time. We'd better hurry.'

In some places, on the way to the cottage, she had idly trailed a piece of driftwood behind her, drawing loops and whirls on the clean damp sand, half-circles like the rope of a hangman's noose. Now, on the return journey, she scuffed these scars with her feet, obliterating the patterns, tearing up the sand so that, when she looked back finally, the mark of her passage looked like the backbone of a mythical creature, huge and marvellous, marked on the lonely margins of the sea.

'Do you remember,' said Louise as they climbed in the car again, 'all those games you children used to play? Do you remember the big red beach ball? And the quoits? And the beach races you used to have? And how someone always had an old box Brownie and took photographs of everyone?'

'No,' she said. 'I don't remember any of that. I don't think I was there.'

Twelve

A LONG TIME AGO, years ago, once in the very early morning before it was light, the telephone pealed in the old house, the noise shrilling up the stairs and into all the bedrooms. From these, faintly, came the sound of small awakenings.

The dolls' pram still stood beneath the curtains on the middle landing then, and the stair carpet was the old floral runner with its burgeoning clusters of bluebells and roses winding endlessly round all the bends, down to the entrance hall where the big red telephone stood on its own shelf.

From the front bedroom the faint murmurings became even fainter, diminishing altogether as Louise sped, naked, down the stairs. 'It's for me,' she nearly shouted, the cousins sleeping in the best room subsiding then into complete silence. *It's for her. For that Louise. At this hour of the day, if you please. Who would it be? Ringing at this time? Waking us all up? What's the time? Barely five o'clock. What madman would ring now? And then, more sleepily, have you put that sapphire ring in a safe place?* They slept with the acute exhaustion of people who have showed themselves off all day in bright sunlight while wearing expensive clothing perhaps too hot for the weather and with large rings purchased at differing times and not necessarily matching.

The calls usually were for Louise, then. She was beautiful. There were race meetings, dances, picnics, dinners. It was race week and people had come to stay. High summer had arrived, with humid nights and cloying days, the temperature always so dizzying that they all slept with the upstairs windows wide open, lace curtains fluffing faintly in any breeze that could be caught and her own secret view — Stephanie's view — of the backyard filled with the luxuriant leaves of the old grapevine, its fruit hanging luscious and swollen with ripeness for the blackbirds and thrushes to eat.

When the telephone began to ring she climbed out of her hoop-backed bed and went along the narrow little passageway to the main landing where the floral carpet began. Familiar occupation made her step high in the darkness to avoid tripping on the mat that lay on the bare boards. The noise had seemed like that of her alarm clock, like some clarion to announce the beginning of work, so she had stepped out of her bed and along the hall still almost asleep, then stood leaning against the wall as she awakened properly, listening to the sounds of the house. The cousins who had gold in their teeth even when they were children had grown up now and wore rouge, tick-tacking smartly around the house in high shoes that had metal points on the end of four-inch heels. They had powder compacts that were sterling silver and might have been bought in London, or anywhere, and from these they extracted little powder puffs to touch up their faces.

'Don't I look awful.'

'No, you look super.' They had their own language, their own terminology, from which she had always felt excluded, even when they were all children, the separation becoming more marked as they all grew older.

'Is she coming to the races,' they would say even if she were right there, standing beside them, 'with us?'

'No, I have to go to work.' Her reproofs were usually undetected.

'Why do you always wear grey?' Sometimes they might speak to her directly. 'My mother says it's an unlucky colour.'

'I like it.' It is the colour of a sky before a storm, she wanted to say, of the margins of the sea, of diamonds at dawn.

'How peculiar.' They would be turning away then to touch up lips already carmine. 'Why do you have to go to work?'

'Because I have to.'

'Can't you get the day off?'

'No, it isn't my turn.'

'I wouldn't work anywhere like that, like wherever it is you work. If I work anywhere I'm going to work in a place where I can have a day off whenever I like. I simply couldn't go every day. What happens if you want to go out somewhere? Oh yes. We forgot.' They seemed to pull themselves up then, like horses. 'Sorry. They said we had to say we were sorry about your mother. Was she sick long? Poor thing. How long will you be staying? Oh really? Just till you find another place — well, good luck.'

The silence in the house after they had all gone was a miracle, when finally the last car drove away with the last pubescent cousin accompanying the last handsome, well-upholstered mother and she was left amid the breakfast dishes and the forgotten race books, the telephone perhaps ringing with one last message. They've all gone, she would say, and they won't be back for hours. Not for hours and hours. And I don't know how you could get hold of them. Sorry. And I'm going to work soon so I can't help you, I'm sorry. The click of the red telephone receiver back on its lurid cradle was as satisfying a sound as her own footsteps threading quietly through the place as she got ready for work, for an office where a lot of what she did was on the telephone, the people removed from her sight, just disembodied voices that were not difficult to cope with. Her notes of the conversations were always immaculate, her tones always moderate and well-modulated.

'Could we speak to that girl with the very pleasant voice,' callers would ask, 'that one who rang last week?' So she was promoted, given a better office.

The morning of the very early telephone call she stood in the shadows of the upper landing, waking up, listening to the noises of the house, the creaking of the old stairs as Louise, naked, hurried down. Then there were the murmured sentences filtering upwards, muffled laughter, the call ending. It was too early to be up, yet too late to go back to bed and start sleeping again. In half an hour her own alarm clock would begin to ring. She had wrapped herself in a silk dressing gown, deep red with a paisley pattern, that she had found in the wardrobe of the little back room. Perhaps another earlier visitor had left it there. It did not seem to belong to anyone so she had borrowed it, wrapping herself in its old luxurious folds, the tassels of its belt falling nearly to her feet.

Yes, no. She could hear Louise's soft voice, Louise's soft laughter, daring yet faintly apprehensive. Yes, that would be lovely. I'd love to. All right, then. Seven o'clock it is. I'll watch out the front windows for you.

What sort of car have you got now? Oh I see. Of course. I'll watch out for a taxi then. Cheerio. Yes, of course I remember. The voice was faint but ripe with promise.

Then there was Louise coming up the stairs again now, her breasts large and luscious like the fruit outside in the garden, her legs tanned from summer days spent at the beach house, her hair golden, lips still smiling in faint triumph, her large eyes shining, toenails lacquered scarlet.

'No need for a fuss.' Already she was speaking as she reached the top landing, breasts bouncing, buttocks like peaches. It was a house where fusses were legendary. Where have you been? Who were you with? What did you do? Who was there? What did they say? 'It was just Tony ringing from Sydney to ask me to have dinner with him tonight. He's flying over today. Go back to sleep. Everyone go back to sleep.' And the door to her room, the one she had slept in since she was a child, slammed on the house, on the stairs, on them all.

'I never heard of anything so ridiculous.' That was Louise's mother, in a salmon pink lockknit nightdress, outside her own bedroom door just before she slammed it as well.

At lunchtime Louise stood in a white tailored suit, the feet shod in high-heeled court shoes, a cigarette between two scarlet-tipped fingers, leaning on the mantelpiece of the old fireplace in the sitting room, a refugee from her own large office down in the middle of town where she managed a company. She had been summoned by the aunts, by the cousins, by everyone.

'There's no need for the Spanish Inquisition,' she was saying. 'He's that chap I used to go out with and then he was transferred to Sydney by his firm. He's just going to be here for tonight on business, that's all, and we're going out to dinner. I wish to heaven you wouldn't make such a fuss, all of you. And it was nearly six o'clock when the telephone rang so who cares about the time. Stephanie stayed up, didn't you?'

'Yes,' she had said from the doorway into the kitchen, a tomato sandwich in her hand, a refugee from another sort of office at the other end of town, an expert at a quick lunch. 'I think it was after six, really.' Another lie. 'I had to go to work early so I stayed up. It was okay.'

'And Stephanie isn't angry, are you? Stephanie isn't put out.'

No, she was not put out. No, she wasn't angry. And then, with the ridiculous impertinence of the very afraid, of the absurdly shy, she had said, 'And I think Louise should be allowed to go out to dinner with Tony.' She spoke fiercely, in fear, as if she knew him, knew what it was all about. 'She's old enough to decide where she can go. She's thirty. People of thirty can go out to dinner if they like. They don't always have to stay home with everyone else.'

In the evening she was the only one to wave goodbye from a house stiff with unuttered fears, from a window whose venetian blind suddenly felt like two dozen razor blades strung on cord, for they were possessive, all of them, and never let things go. When the horses died they were never sold for horse meat to the knacker. One of the uncles got out a bulldozer and buried them on one of the farms.

The grotesqueries of horrible facts are never forgotten. There is always someone who remembers. Think of the man at the service station, the one who bent down to say something through the car window. Was he going to ask if the oil in the motor needed checking? Or was he going to say, 'Don't I remember you? Haven't I seen your face somewhere? Haven't I seen your picture in the paper somewhere?' And slowly it would come to him, perhaps over a day or two. The crime. The victim. The murderer. The facts of crimes, written on court documents, are a form of memory, the voices now silent, the eyes closed.

'It's all your fault,' my aunt said when Louise's marriage went sour. 'You were the one who encouraged her. It was criminal what you did, encouraging her like that. If it hadn't been for you,' she said 'taking her part when she went out to dinner with him that night she might never have gone at all. But for you it might never have happened. If you hadn't taken her part she might never have gone. Before that night she'd never answered back, never once in her life.'

'Even though she was thirty?'

'Even though she was thirty. So it's all your fault. Every bit of it — all your fault entirely.'

From far away my cousin wrote to me, the letters always on thin airmail paper soft as dreams, the stamps brightly coloured, sometimes nearly bizarre. Some were triangular and luminous, I remember. Photographs showed her thinner, slightly anxious. In one she appeared to have a dark bruise on the side of her face, but it could have been the shadow of her hat. The picture was slightly out of focus, blurred as if the hand that held it shook a little, or the photographer was inattentive. Oil drilling is finishing here, she would write in her careful round hand. The Americans are all pulling out now and going back to Texas. There are not a lot of people at the club these days. My friend Trixie — she's the one I told you about in my last letter, the one I played bridge with as my partner — well, she's gone back to Dallas with Fred now. I have got a new amah and she seems to be better than the last one. I quite liked the last one, really, but she took such a lot of stuff that I had to let her go. They all take things, of course, but she took such a lot she had to go, Tony said. This new one seems quite good. We gave a party the other night for some of the expats going home and she coped very well, I thought. The evening was the usual riot. They do change with the drink, the men. You notice that here. People change with the heat and the drink.

In the old house now, she stands in the very early morning at my bedroom door, wraith-like in her silk robe.

'I brought you a cup of tea, Stephanie. I hope it's not too early.'

'Not at all,' I say as I struggle up from the grip of the mattress and the soft pillows. 'Your hair looks nice. I'm glad we went and had it done.'

'Is there anything you want?' they said to me in the morning, after I had slept fully clothed. 'Someone'll bring you some breakfast in a minute. If you have any food allergies just let him know and he'll bring something else.'

'Oysters,' I said.

'What?' The young constable who brought the tray later looked at me with distaste as if I were a sly bird sliding through the updraughts in a sky wild with shot.

'I'm allergic to oysters,' I said and I sat there on that bunk with my legs swung out and over the edge to the floor, my feet planted squarely like those of a workman ready to face a long day.

'We don't serve oysters for breakfast.'

'I'm sure you don't. I was only joking. They said —' But he had already gone, that small glimpse I had of him through part of the door, had gone. One shoulder, a narrow face, a hand holding a small tray, all gone.

Later he gave evidence at the trial.

'Defendant showed no sign of remorse. The following morning when

I was instructed to take her some breakfast — no policewoman being available for the task due to work overload in the Family Court and also a domestic incident being investigated from the station at that exact time — I found her sitting in what seemed to me to be a nonchalant manner on the edge of the bunk in the holding cell. As I watched her through the viewing window, prior to handing her the food, she was combing her hair with her fingers. Later I saw her dampen her handkerchief with some water from her beaker and, while I watched, she wiped her face and hands with this. She seemed calm and unworried. She asked for a mirror. This request was declined due to regulations. As far as I recall, the prisoner said, 'What the heck,' when I explained this to her. She said, 'So I'll just have to have a dirty face then.' When I gave her the food she made what I would term a joke about being allergic to oysters and began to smile when I told her oysters were not served for breakfast to prisoners held in the overnight cells. "I was only joking," she said. "Just tell me anyone who does serve oysters for breakfast." Her attitude seemed to be flippant.

'When I recounted this story later to one of the duty constables from the previous evening he said that when asked about the weapon in question (exhibit 46B) she said to him, "I've already told you. I brought it with me in that parcel I handed in at the desk. It was wrapped up in a teatowel and then brown paper. Ask them at the front desk if they've got a parcel wrapped up in brown paper that a woman handed in last night. It must be there somewhere. What more do you expect me to do. Hand it all to you on a plate? And carry you to it?" Defendant then swore at the constable. "If you can't look after a goddamn parcel that some goddamn woman hands in to you tame as ninepence, what the hell can you do, you stupid bastard?" she said. According to records held at the station it was by then after three o'clock in the morning so the defendant could have been overtired and may possibly have overreacted due to exhaustion. There was still no sign of remorse.'

'I heard you calling out in the night,' said Louise. 'It was about three o'clock. I think I heard the town clock strike three just before I heard you call out. I came in but you were asleep. I think you were dreaming. You said something but I couldn't understand the words.'

'Oh, I often dream.' I took the cup of tea from her. 'You shouldn't come up the stairs with tea for me. You could call me from the kitchen door and I'd come down.' She stood there looking at me, faintly questioning or perhaps, like me, was dazed with sleep. 'Oysters,' I said. 'I dream of harmless things like oysters or parcels or breakfast or anything. Nothing to worry about. I'm sorry I disturbed you. If it happens again just wake me up. Shake my shoulder. I leave the bedroom door open — just come straight in and wake me up. Shout at me. Anything. But just wake me up.'

'You never say anything about yourself.' She was still standing by my bed but looked out the window now, as if removal to the garden, even by view alone, would make speaking easier. 'We could drive past your old house one day if you'd like. Perhaps some of the people you used to know — well, they might still live here. People don't move away from here much. You were the exception, you might remember. You could go off by yourself, Stephanie, and you could visit old friends. I'd be fine here by myself for an afternoon or an evening.'

I sipped the tea slowly, like medicine.

'I've forgotten it all,' I said. 'I never think about it. It's gone from my mind.' And I lay back against the old thin pillows, comfortable with my own lies. 'Perhaps I sometimes dream about oysters because we used to find broken oyster shells on the beach.' I got her talking about holidays a long time ago, about the old cottage and the picnics there, about lots of things. She went downstairs to find the photograph album and I heard her singing as she went.

Thirteen

MURDERS. MURDERERS.

There was this man in California called Abel Waxman who was the last American murderer to die in the gas chamber. After that the method of execution was changed to lethal injection because the gas chamber was deemed inhumane.

He held up a woman, a thirty-seven-year-old nurse, with a knife and demanded her purse. She said, 'I've only got twenty dollars but you can have it — just let me go.' He said, 'Give me more.' She said, 'I haven't got any more, you son-of-a-bitch. It's not payday till tomorrow and I've got to get home to my mother because she's in a wheelchair and she expects me home round five every afternoon. If I'm not there she'll worry. Just take the twenty dollars, it's all I've got, and let me go, please. If it was tomorrow I could give you more. Do you think I go round all week with my pay in my pocket? Get real. Just take the twenty dollars and let me go.' 'You'll die for that,' he said. 'I hate sassy women. No one calls me a son-of-a-bitch. I sentence you to death.' He then stabbed her twenty-eight times. After many stays of execution ranging over a thirteen-year period, he went to the gas chamber.

At the last hearing his lawyer said they could ask for another stay, on technical grounds, but Abel Waxman said, 'No, let's get the show off the road, buddy boy. I want to die. Just let me die.' The judge said, 'Do you know what you're saying?' Waxman said, 'Okay, yes, I know what I'm saying. I'm saying I just want to die. I've had enough of this. Just bring me a hooker for my last request.' Judge: 'If that is your last request it will have to be declined. The court cannot grant requests of this kind.'

Waxman: 'So I can't have a hooker? But what I really want is a hooker. This is my last request I'm talking about here. Just bring me a hooker and let me die. That's all I ask.' Judge: 'I'm afraid the judicial system is unable to comply with requests of this kind. Could you ask for something else.' 'Okay,' said Abel Waxman, 'let me have my last meal then. I want to die. It's not in me to stick around for the next ten years. I want to die.' Judge: 'Now, you know that the choice you're making here is life or death. Do you understand that?' Waxman: 'I understand. I choose death. Let me have my last meal, then, if I can't have a hooker. Bring me a hamburger, with cheese and fries, no sauce, not lamb, must be lean beef fine-ground twice, onions and plenty of fries. And I like the bun toasted on one side. But not toasted is okay if toasting's a problem. Just let me have my last meal and let me die. I want this show off the road. But if you change your mind about the hooker you'll know where I am, Cell 46, third on the left, but if I can't have the hooker, let me have the hamburger. And remember, plenty of fries. Let's get the ball rolling.'

Teresa Findlay, aged six, was beaten by her father so often and so brutally that her abdomen was swollen as if she were pregnant. He threw her against the kitchen table and when the edge of the top cut her head open to the bone he sewed up the wound with an ordinary needle and thread. He held her under the water in the toilet and the bath frequently till she was on the point of drowning. He poked his fingers in her eyes. On the night he finally killed her, by throttling, he placed her body in a black plastic rubbish sack and buried it in the woods in an unmarked grave. It was never found. He steadfastly refused to divulge its whereabouts throughout his fifteen years on death row and on the day when he was finally executed he was asked for the last time where Teresa was buried. Legal documents state his reply as being profanities. Defendant uttered profanities. That is all.

You can read about any of these things, these occurrences, in newspapers and magazines with bright covers. People give magazines and books for Christmas. The people don't want them so they put them in bags to be distributed to institutional libraries. So you end up reading someone's Christmas present yourself, by accident. *To Dad with love from Marge and the kids. Hope the year's been good to you.* It comes upon your eyes as a surprise when your hand turns the page without any suspicion that, over the leaf, will be a heading — 'Reminiscences of a

Hanging Judge', 'Murderers I Saw to the Death Chamber', 'A Life for a Life'.

California again. Alton Harris confessed to killing two teenage boys on the exact day he committed the crime. His confession was never delayed. It was spontaneous, exact, rapid. He said he wanted their car. It was as simple as that. After they were both dead he ate the hamburgers they had purchased a short time before. One had three bite marks in it. The other was half eaten. That boy had always been a quick eater, a gobbler. His mother used to tell him about it. 'Stop eating that quick, Bobber,' she would say. 'One day you sure as hell will choke yourself, boy.' He died without a sound. The other boy saw the man with the gun and gave a cry as Harris aimed. Afterwards Harris ate the hamburgers. The meat was not rare but there was blood on one bun. With stays of execution and the usual runaround by lawyers it was fifteen years before he was finally strapped down to await the dropping of the sodium cyanide pellets into the sulphuric acid. At a little after six o'clock in the morning on the day of his execution he began to inhale deeply the deadly gas while relatives of his victims watched from six feet away. They were seated in an observation room that had recently been redecorated in pastel shades and had upright chairs, like dining chairs in an ordinary house. These were upholstered, also ordinarily, in a linen fabric known by the codename Sage 46/9° in decorating folders containing swatches.

There was another murderer, a woman, who killed her lover and then went and found her father. She climbed through the window of his room in a home for old men and she stood there, on the mat beside his chair. 'Who are you?' he said. He was reading the newspaper. 'I'm your daughter,' she said. 'I haven't seen you since you were nine,' he said. 'How do I know you're my daughter? I suppose you want money, do you? All you bitches of women are the same. All you want is money.' 'No,' she said, 'I don't want money. And as for being your daughter, I'll prove it to you if you don't believe me.' She lit a match. 'Do you remember,' she said, 'how, when I was a little girl, you used to burn me with matches? Do you recall how you used to put methylated spirits on my arms so they'd burn better? See what it feels like, you bastard. Do you remember that game you liked so much — that game where you tortured me with burning matches but I wasn't allowed to move or cry out and if I did you burnt me again? Do you remember that? Fun, wasn't it? You used to call it funning, I remember. Shall we have another lovely game of funning?' In the end he begged to die. His room was isolated. The staff were dilatory. It was a cheap place. People often made a noise because they were drunk. She did not actually kill him. He had a heart attack from terror and exhaustion. When she heard the death rattle in his throat she kicked his shins and said, 'Die, you bastard.' Then she climbed out the window again and caught a bus. 'Good afternoon,' she said to the driver, 'super day, isn't it?'

Fourteen

A *SEPIA PHOTOGRAPH* of a wedding group, two earnest bridesmaids faintly alike as if they might have been cousins or sisters, both wearing cloche hats on smooth hair. Once again it is midnight and I am exploring the varied small entertainments of the dressing table. The bridesmaids are wearing ivory satin shoes with Louis heels, each pair of feet carefully placed, toes pointed. Now, ladies and gentlemen, all as graceful as possible, please. That is the photographer speaking from behind his tripod. Do we have all those toes pointed? Elbows in? All your bouquets at the right angle? All smile then — lovely. Snap. There is the picture — the bride with her head tilted slightly to one side, the expression quizzical, her own cloche hat worked in a fancier stitch than the others, the cream lace of her dress skimming a slim girl's body and the eyes large and dark and questioning. And what do you have in store for me world, life, everybody? The poke bonnet of a grim dour child partially obscured the bridal bouquet, the view of its lilies sliced down the middle by the sharp little brim, significant as an interrupted remark. I will always look after y — I will always love y — Like that — just snap in the middle and the words might have stopped, the lilies cut off, obscured by the sudden dull lump of the child's hat. All the bouquets so large they looked full of springing untrimmed vines, ferns assembled whole, entire lily plants wrenched from the tender ground on the morning of the wedding to cascade in a floral frenzy from gloved hands, most dresses nearly obscured by the greenery, all the people just big, dark eyes, smooth heads, neat ankles in little ivory shoes, nothing much to be seen between the heads and the shoes except that sliver of the bride's dress. Everyone, even the sulky little girl, standing against a backdrop so dim it looked like the mouth of endless time, the entry to a lost campagna with no bridegroom, no groomsmen, no men at all as if, like shepherdesses, the girls planned their own festivities in a demesne full of scents and flowers and children, forever faintly amused, dark-eyed and innocent.

'Whose is the old wedding photograph on the dressing table?' I ask in the morning.

'It's your mother's. That was your mother. I put it there for you. I thought you might like to see it.'

'Who were the bridesmaids? And the flower girl?'

My cousin goes to the dressing table and picks up the picture.

'I think they were cousins,' she said. 'They were probably cousins. I think I remember hearing that they were cousins from out in the country, from a farm, and they all made their own dresses. They used to talk on the telephone about how the frills would be but when they all met up on the wedding day everyone had done their frills a bit differently. They all had sewing machines and they made their own dresses. Did I hear you up late again last night? I thought I heard your window open.' The change in subject is swift and forbidding, but I persist.

'Why aren't there any men in the picture?'

'There were. That was just an extra picture taken of all the girls. It seems,' says my cousin and her voice is like an invisible wall, a gate that says NO TRESPASSERS, 'to be the one Mother preferred, the one she kept.'

'I see.' And I think I do. I think I do see what she means. The good men died. The bad ones ran away with the red-headed wives of other bad men. Why keep their photographs?

Much later in the morning we go on our daily circuit of the garden, which is on a higher level than the street, built up by old stone walls and hedged, at the front, by rhododendrons gone woody. Stinging winds from the lonely margins of the sea whip in there, drying the leaves and withering flowers.

Brackish geraniums with clusters of brittle leaves rustle faintly in the breeze that always flickers around the front lawn.

'Hello, Louise.' A voice comes through the trees. Someone walking along the street has seen us, has seen the dressing-gowned form of Louise and I feel her hand tighten on my arm.

'Don't tell anyone I'm sick, will you, Stephanie.'

'Not if you don't want me to.'

'Hello? Hello? Is that you, Louise?' The voice is determined and we turn bright, bland faces towards the caller. Everyone for blocks around the old house knows Louise is called Louise and that she has lived in that house since she was a little girl. It is a suburb where people stay, where estates are left to favourite nieces or widowed daughters and then the niece or the daughter lives in that place till she dies, and so it goes on. There is continuity in the area as though the account of their lives is embroidered on an endless hanging with all loose threads neatly sewn in, the figures embroidered in satin stitch, then a changeover to chain stitch quickly to form the outlines of dwellings, of shops and sheds. Little Louise with her bucket and spade at the old beach cottage. Louise growing bigger and older. Louise a beautiful girl. A smaller child, a little unsmiling girl in a kitchen, regarding her with admiration so marked it is almost a tangible thing. Big girl/little girl. The little girl writing an essay at school — 'What I Did in the Holidays'. In the holidays I went to see my aunt and uncle and my cousin Louise. My cousin Louise wears lovely dresses and goes out a lot. I love to sit at the top of the stairs and watch her going out in her pretty clothes. When I grow up I want to be like Louise. Louise a woman at that peculiar age when women become invisible to others, neither old nor young, just invisible. The garden. The spade leaning against the front verandah. The gnarled old trees. The caller. All done in wild loops of chain stitch, some uneven.

'I haven't seen you for a while, Louise. Are you all right? Have you been away on holiday?' The caller is not going to be repelled by the silence. She advances on flat, determined feet.

'Don't let her come near me, Stephanie. I just don't want to see anyone. I don't want anyone to see me.' And there is that arm again, guarding the chest, a bar of secrecy against intrusion for that tailored lack of flesh, those little bars of surgical tape that hold the edges of wounds together.

'Go inside. Run, run.' And there is Stephanie, me, embroidered in the mythical tapestry of life in red satin stitch to show a scarlet jersey, pushing Louise. 'Run.'

'Is that you, Louise?' The gate is creaking. The caller enters.

'No, it's only me. Louise is just a bit tired. She's resting. We were looking at the garden for a moment. She heard the telephone so she's gone inside to answer it. May I introduce myself.' And I don't. That's the funny thing. No one ever notices that I don't ever say who I am, not exactly. 'I'm Louise's cousin from out of town. I've just popped in for a few days. How nice to meet you.' How quickly the crop of lies grows.

What do you do out in the garden, Stephanie? I've been told you stand there for hours, brooding. This is the man with the notebook again, the doctor who reads novels. I'm fine. I was just thinking. I don't think I was out there for that long, was I? Oh sorry. Gosh, was it that long? I won't do it again. Must have gone off into a little daydream and forgot the time. No, no, nothing's wrong. I'm absolutely fine. Yes, I sleep well. Yes, I feel really cheerful. Nothing to worry about at all, thank you. Good of you to enquire.

'Are you the one I've heard about?'

'Probably.'

'Oh.' The figure is suddenly stationary. All movement ceases. The feet are planted squarely on the front path in shoes so sensible, so large they could be the boxes that held them rather than actual footwear. 'Well, tell her I called.' She turns one last time before going quickly out the gate. 'I thought you'd be older. From the photographs in the paper I thought you'd be older.'

'Thank you.' I feel this is inadequate, but what can I say.

'What did she want?' In the kitchen the kettle is humming again. During the day we live on cups of tea and bread and butter and an occasional tomato sandwich at odd times though Louise always has her porridge for breakfast. In the evenings I cook splendid meals of roast chicken with fine herbs and potatoes au gratin and we sit in the kitchen laughing like two old women having a party. 'Thanks for getting rid of that old cat.'

'That's okay. She was probably just a bit intrigued, that's all. She seemed to know who I was. I said I was your cousin.'

'Well, you are. You are my cousin. What's the matter with that?'

'Nothing.' There's nothing wrong with being Louise's cousin, it is what kind of cousin I am/was.

'Eat your sandwich.' So we sit there, in that redecorated kitchen that is lit by the sun in the mornings and if we were to be embroidered again in the tapestry there we would be, done in yellow and holding little striped sandwiches in pink satin stitch hands.

And, earlier in the tapestry, there would be Louise, a brilliant bride in pale blue lace and wearing an eighteen-carat platinum engagement ring shaped like a bow set with sapphires, all large, with a wedding band to match. Louise leaving the airport with a graduated set of tartan suitcases and matching dressing case, the red and blue threads very bold now, labels fluttering on the handles. London. Paris. Hamburg. Berlin. New York. Hong Kong. Singapore. Louise returning home one winter when the river burst its banks and houses down the street were flooded up to the kitchen ceilings for the first time in living memory. Just one tartan suitcase now, the big sapphire ring kept in its box in a drawer and never worn again. The wool and silks in darker colours now. Grey, black, browns, the sombre colours of autumn. Thank you for calling. Louise isn't very well at the moment. She's upstairs resting. I'll give her your regards. That is Louise's mother speaking but she is dead now and I have the same lines as if we are in an endless play with the same dialogue uttered by different characters at different times.

'Today,' I say, 'we might go back to the beach if you feel like it.'

Fifteen

THE CLOCK STRUCK one down in the hall, the shadows of the night falling on the faded wallpaper of fruit and flowers. She went to the window again, swung the casement out as far as it would go, a wide arc into the silence. From far away, the town clock echoed one. Slip-slop endlessly through time, a minute late, a minute early.

'You're early,' she had said the last time she had dinner with him and her mind, now, went slip-slop over the exact time, the precise assemblage of numbers that might date it all accurately. It was the year the autumn colours were so bold, the year of the two hurricanes, the year before she had seen her own pale face in the curdled old mirror of the chiffonier. 'I wasn't expecting you quite so soon. Just come in for a minute. I'm not quite ready.' She never kept him waiting, had never kept him waiting before that night. She had stood aside in the narrow old doorway, the hall behind her also long and narrow and cold as a sword. Or perhaps, she thought now as she leaned out into the night, it was like one of the lilies in the wedding portrait, a narrow trumpet leading out into the wide petals of the flowery living room with her climbing roses tapping on the windows.

'Just come in and sit down for a moment. Can I get you a drink? Would you like to look at this?' And she handed him a *Time* magazine.

'You look fine to me.' He put the magazine down on the floor and looked at his watch. Not at her, she thought later, only at his watch. 'Just hurry. No need to fuss. Just come as you are. There's not a lot of time, Stephanie. I'm not sure when she's coming home again. Just come, Stephanie, any old how. Let's get dinner over and done with.'

'You make me sound like a chore. I remember,' she had said, 'when you used to count how many times you'd seen me. I remember when the tally got to ten, then twenty. I remember when you took me out to a special lunch because we'd reached a hundred. I remember when you used to telephone me twice a day to make sure I was still here and hadn't run away with anyone else. What is the tally now? What is the total now?' Each word in the last two sentences clear as a chopper.

'I've forgotten,' he said. 'Just hurry. I've told you, Stephanie — they're a very temperamental family. They haven't got much common sense. Clever academically, yes, common sense no, Stephanie. I've already had a scene with her today because she cut her hand before she went out and I nearly didn't get her away. She's stopping at some clinic on the way to get a stitch put in, so she says. She might come home again. Stephanie, I don't want to lose everything. If she found out she'd be vindictive. I don't want to lose my house. I don't want to lose any more of my property. I've lost enough already. I've just got the bookshelves put up in my study and the pictures hung. The painters are coming in on Monday to do the ceiling. I don't want to lose it all. Just hurry. I don't care what you look like.' He waited then. 'You always look fine,' he said, but she thought it was a lie.

I kept putting the same clothes on. For a long time I kept putting the same clothes on, always black. She noticed he had begun to write, not in a notebook but on a large A4 pad on the desk. His hand inscribed wide flowing circles like the movements of an artist who draws ripples on a pond. Do you like it here? she asked. You're new, aren't you? I sometimes wonder if people like it here. The silence from outside was suddenly broken by the sound of a lawnmower. Someone had begun to cut the grass between the blocks, the noise of the mower nearly jarring on the teeth. She placed one hand over her left cheek to cover a sudden pain that ran from her eye socket down to her upper jaw. By the same clothes, he said, what exactly do you mean? And that mannerism I notice? Your hand on your face like that? Does that have a meaning? Not really, she said. It's just that noise outside — it just reminds me of once when I was a child, when I was about eight or nine, someone hit me on the cheekbone while the man next door was mowing his lawn. Perhaps we could talk about that another day, he said. Now, today, these clothes you mention. These black clothes. Tell me about the black clothes.

They weren't exactly the same garments day after day, she told him. Not at all. They were not the same exact clothes so they became dirty or anything like that — no. Just the same type of clothes, clothes with the same look, clothes of the same colour. What colour? he asked and she noted that the pen was going faster now, the notations becoming more crisp. Black. I wore black. Like I said, just black. Nothing else, just black. He used to say to me, Oh, another of your Hamlet outfits. I have a very limited knowledge of Shakespeare so it took me a while to sort out what he meant. Hamlet always wore black. Hamlet wore tight hose and a vel-vet jacket with a ruffled collar. Or I think — I thought — that's what Hamlet wore. I used to wear — and she would stop there. I can't really think what I wore. I know I used to stand in front of the wardrobe and I wouldn't know what to put on. I couldn't think what went with what any more, what would match what. I couldn't think. So I just used to put on black clothes because they matched. I'd wear black from head to toe. I'd wear black trousers or black jeans, and a black jersey or a black shirt. I remember, far into the summer that year, I bought some dye at the chemist shop up the road and I redyed a lot of my things. Why? he want-ed to know. Why did you do that? Because they had gone kind of green at the seams, she had told him. They looked a bit shabby. Some had a greyish look. I suppose it depends on the dye or the fabric or on God knows what. So I bought some dye and I redyed them so they'd be crisply black again, so they'd look smart again.

Did you want to look smart? The pen stopped there and she looked into a pair of eyes that looked suddenly full of assessment. I don't know, she had said. I can't remember. I know I felt very pained that I looked shabby, so, yes, I suppose I did want to look smart. Aha, he said. And did this man, this man whom you later killed, did he notice any of this? No, she said. Yes. I don't know. I know he noticed that I had got black dye on my hands. It took a while to wear off. No matter how you put rubber gloves on and do it all very carefully, you still get black dye somehow in the gloves or on your hands so, later, when you have a good look at your-self, all under your fingernails has gone black as if you're dirty, but you aren't. I remember the palms of my hands were quite black. I remember I splashed the dye on the laundry floor, which was covered in white linoleum, and I never got the stains off. I remember a lot of things about that summer.

'Snap,' he had said when she came out of her bedroom. 'Another of your little Hamlet outfits. Righto then? Are we ready to go?' There had been something relentless about the set of his shoulder blades through the linen jacket, something resigned about the angle of his head as he tramped up the hall towards her front door.

'If you don't want to go,' she said as she climbed in the car, 'you don't have to. I'm not like the dentist or anything. You don't have to do anything you don't want to. I'd sooner know. I'd sooner you said. I'm used to being at home,' she said, 'by myself. It really doesn't worry me, not any more. I'd sooner be at home by myself than out where I'm not welcome.'

'Just move some of that stuff off the seat — yes, just throw it on the floor. There's plenty of room. Now just slide in there. That's fine.' He gave no sign of having heard. She glanced down at her shoes as he started the car, but they were not too muddy. There had been rain the previous night and the grass verge was still sodden, clamping her high heels in a glutinous grip. 'If you wore sensible shoes you wouldn't have that problem.' So he had noticed her concern, he had perceived where her looks fell, and, for a moment, she had been reassured. He took a deep breath. 'Oh good,' he said, 'you haven't got that very strong perfume on. It does linger, you know. I wish you wouldn't wear it, not in the car. I think the dog smells it but, fortunately, dogs can't talk. What did you tell me it was called?'

'Bonzo,' she said.

'No, not the dog, the perfume.'

'Poison,' she said. 'The perfume's called Poison.' She was silent for the rest of the journey .

'That was a lovely quiet ride,' he said when he had found a parking place over the road from the café.

'Wasn't it?' she said. 'And I can't wear it any more' — they were crossing the road now, ducking between the oncoming traffic — 'because it's run out. I haven't got any more and it's too expensive for me to buy now. I can't afford it. So tell your goddamn dog not to be concerned.'

'Sometimes, Stephanie,' he said, 'I don't know what you're talking about.' But they had reached the kerb by then and he was already looking towards the open doors of an Italian place with vines growing over the windows. 'I thought spaghetti,' he said. 'For a change.'

'Oh goody. Worms. Just what I like.'

'One thing I do like about you,' he said, 'is that really sick, slick sense of humour of yours. Sometimes, Stephanie, you do make me laugh. And the dog's called Fred.' And while she watched him, in her tight black trousers and the black velvet jacket because she couldn't think what to wear, he did begin to laugh. At her. He began to laugh at her.

If you could cast your mind back to that summer, he said as he continued to write those wide, generous letters like ripples in a pond, tell me what you remember about it most. What is your most valid memory of that summer? My most valid memory of that summer is that I haven't a proper memory of it at all. I think everything I thought was wrong, everything I did was wrong. I don't think I remember it properly at all. It seems, to me, that what I remember is right but I think it must be wrong. I think I must have been wrong. Perhaps, she said, if I had been able to go away. If I had gone away on that holiday the other man used to talk to me about, that one who was here before you. He used to say if I had, perhaps, been able to go away on a holiday for three or four weeks I would have felt better. Do you believe that? She watched the pen stop. No, but I might have felt differently and, under the circumstances, that might have passed for feeling better.

In the invisible spaces of sleep, things I will not contemplate during the day come out to populate the empty reaches of the night. There is still the business of the lost hour and a half. They sometimes said that, perhaps about once or twice a year towards the end. Perhaps they gave up. The lost hour and a half, I'd say. Don't you mean one hour and thirty-five minutes exactly? Okay, so it was exactly one hour and thirty-five minutes. At this very late date do you have anything you'd like to say about it? I've already told you. I've probably said it thousands of times. I might have fainted. I might have stood there transfixed and thought it was only a moment and it was an hour and a half. There's that famous American Civil War story, that one about the man from Owl Creek who was hung from a bridge and the rope broke as he fell so he swam over to the other side of the river and escaped over the countryside to be reunit-

ed with his loving wife. She came running down the steps of their house with her arms outstretched to meet him so gladly. And at that instant he reached the full extent of the rope's length, his neck broke and he died. He had imagined it all in the second between his fall and his death. I might have imagined, in a kind of reverse scenario, that I stood there transfixed for just a moment in terror and it was an hour and thirty-five minutes. Untrue, of course. There was only one of them I felt a qualm about deluding, and that was the first man with the notebook, the one who talked to me about books. But I know what I did in those ninety-five minutes and I can tell you I was moving swiftly all the time and it was necessary to do so to cover the area, to get where I wanted to go and back again. No one ever said they saw me which I found — I find — odd because my appearance was noted, I remember that. There was a bus driver who looked at my shoes as he gave me change for my ticket and I said, terse and telegrammatic, 'Supermarket,' and jerked one hand over my shoulder towards a shopping mall a block away. 'Butchery,' I said. 'Gets a bit messy. Hoping for a better job soon.' 'Don't tell me about it, lady,' he said, and handed me my change. 'These days you gotta do what you gotta do.' 'Indeed,' I said and I just went down to about the middle of the bus and sat down.

There's always someone who'll tell you things you don't want to know. There's always the chance encounter in the street, the best friend of a long-lost cousin who'll say, 'Aren't you related to the Baileys? Wasn't your father the one who was such a devil with women? I bet your mother had to nail him down. Funny thing — I was just talking about him the other day and someone said he's eighty-three now if he's a day and he's got sugar diabetes and he's in some rest home in Cherrybrook Avenue over Mount Albert way.' There's always someone who'll tell you. They love to tell you anything that causes immense distress going back to earliest infancy, news that might send you home sick at heart even after all this time, after all those years, they love to tell you such things. 'Do you go to see him? You don't? And he's your own father. Fancy not ever going to see your own father. You ought to be ashamed.' You stand there, dumb on some bus stop, in the entrance to some department store somewhere, in a street where the wind suddenly starts to blow rough and cold. And you felt all right till then. You felt quite smart, quite nicely dressed, quite educated from all the courses over the years, all the reading, all the clearly enunciated fine sweet syllables, all the soap, thousands of baths, hundreds of haircuts, miles of toothpaste, several dentists, truckloads of antibiotics, oceans of medicine, health insurance of the better sort, an engraved lapel badge saying you are the head of a department, an engraved lapel badge saying you are the wife of the managing director, a Visa Gold Card. You felt just fine, till then.

Silence is a clear message. I knew an old doctor who told me that. Yet you can stand there silently and it passes for guilt. 'Fancy not going to see your own father.' Silence. It seems like dereliction and delinquency. Once I said, 'He could have remembered that at the time possibly, don't you think?'

Cherrybrook Avenue was a well-known street. Things might be different now. Perhaps the main road to the western suburbs has been diverted over kinder countryside, perhaps the junction with Cherrybrook Avenue is in a backwater now, a mossy byway with its sign falling down. At the time about which I write it had a huge sign right over the road, above the traffic lights. Cherrybrook Avenue Bypass, Heavy Traffic. It was easy enough to find. I'd seen it dozens of times. And a rest home for the elderly is also easy to locate. I knew the address already. You look in the yellow pages of the telephone book when you arrive home feeling sick with ancient horrors and there it is, predictably called the Cherrybrook Rest Home, listed in alphabetical order, stated in neat capitals, a boxed entry so the proprietors must have paid an extra fee for a slightly more lavish presentation. And the address is immediately etched on the surface of your brain because that is where he is, perhaps comfortably eating dinner at this very minute, clasping the knee of the night attendant who has learnt to leap spryly out of the way, a man with the full and pouting lower lip of those who have treated themselves well forever and now resent being caged by infirmity.

Each room had one long window looking out over a rancid garden lined with wilted cactus plants and a box tree dying in a pot that had always been too small to hold its roots. I learnt instantly that you can never forget. You can never forget the line of a jaw, the slope of a shoulder, the turn of a head, the lie of a hand. His hands were an old man's hands, putty-coloured and pumice-textured, large, empty hands that looked as if the flesh and the skin were suddenly too big for the bones. I knew him immediately, knew his silhouette instantly, when I walked

118

along the garden path, past those addled cacti, past the cars parked in the drive, the sound of televisions in other rooms, each of which was exactly the same as his and yet his presence in that one room made it blaze for me. I stepped in, over the low sill.

'Who the hell are you?' he said. He was never, for me, a man who had a charm with words.

'Stephanie,' I said.

'Stephanie who?'

'Stephanie who is your daughter,' I said, and I waited. I watched him see me properly, look at me properly. His eyes were small and dark and seemed to have no whites. Perhaps he had cataracts. I don't know. 'Do you know what I've just done?' I said. 'I've just killed someone. I'll show you the knife if you like.' And I got it out of the parcel I had under my arm.

'You're mad,' he said. I thought he looked suddenly afraid. 'I haven't seen Stephanie for years. How do I know you're Stephanie? And what do you want? I'm not giving you any money.' He was always mean, a mean man except with himself.

'I don't want money,' I said, 'and I know you haven't seen me for years. You haven't seen me since I was nine. Do you know,' I said, conversational and nice, as if it were a pleasant picnic, 'when I was nine I used to take things from the house and wrap them up in newspaper and address them to myself on my birthday? I used to pretend that the postman had put them in the letter-box for me and that you had sent them, that you had sent me something for my birthday. Or for Christmas,' I said. I sounded like an obliging shopkeeper, nice, jolly, unperturbed. 'That's what I used to do.'

He sat there, a mound of a man, silent. I noticed his hands had a faint tremor, but old people's hands do tremble. Perhaps his hands always trembled. I remembered when the hands were younger and stronger, when the sound they made was like a board breaking if he hit someone.

'I've got a bad heart,' he said.

'Haven't we all.'

'They've got me on four different pills,' he said. 'Some of them are blue. I'm not allowed to be upset. I could go anytime. They say I'm living on a knife edge. I'm a sick man.'

119

'You are,' I said, 'and that's fine by me. Great. Don't worry. I'm not going to upset you. I'm just going to kill you.' I sat down on the other chair with the knife still in my hand. 'But I'm going to take my time about it,' I said, 'just like you did years ago when you used to make me carry your razor strap around all day before you beat me with it. Do you remember the time,' I said, 'that you tried to run us over in the car? Do you remember that? You were driving very slowly then, I recall — perhaps so Mother and I didn't hear the motor. Was that it?' In the end I just sat there and I watched him die. His own thoughts, his fear, killed him far more quickly than I would have done. He gave a gasp and he slipped slightly sideways in the chair. After a little while I heard a noise from his throat like the sound a person might make gargling, that kind of sound. Then there was nothing. I read in a book once that the death rattle is unmistakable but I thought it sounded very ordinary, like someone gargling.

DID ANYONE SEE THIS WOMAN? *There were pictures of me on Crimewatch for two weeks in a row but no one came forward. The missing ninety-five minutes remained a mystery, remain a mystery. There is an age when women become invisible. It can be curiously and accurately charted from the first time you go into a restaurant and the waiter calls you 'Madam' while he clears away the other place set on the small table for two you have chosen. He knows instinctively that no one else will ever be there. There are seldom tables for one in restaurants. One is a pariah. One is uneconomic. One is unlikely to become garrulous and festive, ordering another bottle of wine and an unaccustomed and expensive dessert. One buys a glass of house red, slowly eats a small steak or fillet of fish with the usual accoutrements while reading in a desultory fashion from a book with short chapters and a bright cover — even a magazine will do — and goes quietly away out the door as the evening hots up. Laughter is coming from other parties. The crowd is growing thicker. Remarks are exchanged between acquaintances sitting at other tables. One pays the bill and goes quietly out the door and the maitre d' does not say goodnight because the departure is unnoticed, even though he has taken the cheque or the cash and stowed it swiftly and decisively in the till. It is the same with bus drivers. An invisible woman with blood on her shoes. Medium height, medium age, medium hair, clothes of medium quality, the belted coat a little worn at the cuffs and coats with belts aren't in at the moment. They were in the year before last or the year before that. One is unnoticed.*

As for my father, I have no idea what happened exactly. I suppose a laconic nurse aide found him at teatime when she brought his tray of food — perhaps tinned tomato soup and fingers of white bread toasted in dark stripes. I suppose a funeral was held. I suppose people from the Cherrybrook Rest Home clubbed together to buy a wreath. I don't know.

DID ANYONE SEE THIS WOMAN? This invisible woman? Brownish hair, medium height, medium age? Dirty shoes? No.

Sixteen

IN THE MORNING she was awakened early by the ringing of the telephone in the downstairs hall. There was no sound from the room next door, no sign of earlier awakenings, no cups of tea left on the bedside table.

The stairs, taken two at a time, made the same creakings she had always remembered, the old wood more shrunken now and the sounds more complaining, more peevish. At the bend on the middle landing, where the stairs turned and went down another long flight towards the old kitchen, she swung quickly and nearly wildly on to the top stair with a hand on the round finial of the wooden newel post, a game forbidden in childhood but instinctively used now.

'Hello?' She had reached the bottom stair, one thin quick hand on the telephone receiver. From upstairs came faint sounds of movement.

'Good morning Mrs —' and the voice stopped. Louise's curiously unpronounceable name often puzzled people and they took refuge in vague murmurings, indecipherable little gushes of breath. 'How are things today?'

'Fine,' she said, and waited for detection, waited to be discovered as an impostor. Then, in that peculiar awkwardness and volubility engendered by sudden early awakening and immediate consciousness, she said, 'It's a lovely day here today. Slight wind from the east. No hint of rain. A wonderful sky of magical opaqueness with a cloud shaped like a horse and carriage going quietly by at this very minute. I can see it out the stairwell window.'

The caller cleared his throat and there were sounds of movement, perhaps his feet shuffling awkwardly on the floor. He coughed.

'Yes, um, well —' The voice faded away on a falling note, the vowels tumbling into each other like tired cards in a game. 'And how is the patient?' Each word was separate, nothing falling or slurred now, everything official and sharp as if he had the question written on a piece of paper in front of him.

'She's very well,' she said, then realised he did not mean Louise. So, she thought, they called her the patient, did they? 'The patient,' she said with a strengthening mendacity, the vowels round and strong, 'seems very well. The patient is cooking and writing and sleeping and driving the car and shopping and talking normally. She shows,' she said, remembering snatches of conversations overheard on previous mornings, 'no sign of wanting to go away or leave or, indeed, go anywhere unless she's asked to go. Her conversation' — and she was hurrying through the words now, like a killer homing in with the blows, cutting and slashing quickly — 'is completely innocent and is mostly about the dolls in a toy pram that used to be on the landing here when she was a little girl, about flowers and helicopters and making relish and picking roses and —'

'Yes, yes.' The voice was impatient now, eager to escape from the tendrils of delusion woven by a woman far away. 'And you?' he asked. 'I hope all's well with you. You're not frightened?'

'Oh no,' she said, 'I'm fine.' She was smiling now and heard the smile somehow emblazoned upon her voice, printed on it like a warm hand placed fondly on loved flesh. 'I'm really excellent. I haven't felt so well for a long time. I'm not sure what we're going to do today. Perhaps we'll just stay at home. We seem to be happy at home.'

'You sound different today,' he said. 'Better. More robust.'

'I am different.' She waited. 'I am indeed different and more robust.'

When she had placed the receiver carefully back on its cradle she looked up and saw Louise, in a dressing gown, on the upstairs landing.

'I left you sleeping,' she said. 'I told him' — and she nodded her head towards the telephone in a grinning, contemptuous kind of way — 'I was fine and you were behaving well and not showing any sign of wanting to run away.' Surrounded by the sound of Louise's faint, tittering laugh, she turned and went out to the kitchen to make the porridge.

The day passed extravagantly, a profligate expenditure of time on arcane and gentle activities so simple they were almost childish, the afternoon spent in sleep so deep, so undisturbed that when they arose as dusk was falling, it seemed as though they had passed into another time, another season.

In the morning, with the porridge saucepan still unwashed, they had skittered out over the back porch to rearrange the cars in the old garage at the end of the drive, Louise directing and gesturing with her good arm, the other still folded neatly over her chest, always like a wing.

'That's that then.' Stephanie stood with her back to the street, viewing the jigsaw puzzle of the shed with the two cars neatly stowed away, her own in the far corner in a nearly unnegotiable space, and Louise's sitting proudly in front on the cleanest part of the concrete floor. Together she and Louise pressed the button that made the doors come down over it all, masking the secrets of their reticent comings and goings, their tiny expeditions to have a haircut or buy tomatoes. Outside, in the street, came the slow sound of footsteps but the approach to the old house was now empty. Vacant drive, closed gates, no unfamiliar car parked under the golden ginkgo tree, the mark of the tyre treads probably not visible from the street. The footsteps quickened. Disappointed. Nothing to see today. Perhaps that cousin had gone, that one who once lived just down the road in the house that had to be given a new number.

They went indoors together, skittering up the back steps again and over the old porch like children in a careful race, a pretence of speed and effervescence so Louise could be the first to reach the back door.

'First one to the door will live to be a hundred.' She heard her own smile printed on her voice again as Louise slipped inside ahead of her, to the porridge saucepan and the tea cooling in the old teapot, to two teacups painted with pink roses and placed on a little tray as if they belonged there.

Later, at a plant nursery down the road, they purchased an exuberance of parsley in a big square pot, coriander and borage with its big flat leaves and bell flowers of brilliant blue. And honesty, they bought honesty plants in another square container that sat neatly beside the parsley on the back seat of the car like twin thoughts that leave no space for doubt, the starry blue flowers of the borage brilliant and lovely.

Could we just go through it once more? said the blue-eyed policeman. So, after the incident, you say you stood there for an unspecified time, up to an hour and a half, and then you walked along the street and caught the bus to town. Yes, she said. I think that's what must have happened. I feel very tired. I felt very tired. I must have fainted. Perhaps I just went into a dream. But, if you had fainted, your clothes would show signs of this. Your clothes would be stained. My clothes are stained, she said. Indeed yes, your clothes are stained, but not in the right way to denote that you lay on the floor, which you must have done if you had, in fact, fainted and fallen down. Could we continue in the morning, please? I'm too tired. Just another question or two, he said. This difficulty with the timing is something I'd like to explore a little more. But I did it. I've come here to tell you what I did. Surely that's enough, isn't it? He did not answer but she glanced into those brilliant blue eyes, just for an instant, and she saw perfectly that his wall of facts and figures, motives and horrors, had a space in the middle, a missing hour and a half through which doubt and suspicion filtered. Have you ever suffered from a serious illness, he said, or were you taking any drugs at the time? No, she said, never. I'm a very well person usually. When did you last take any kind of medication? Oh, and she had leaned back then in the narrow chair to consider the matter, perhaps about four weeks ago I took a Disprin. Why did you do that? Because I had a headache. And there were those vivid blue eyes again, sharp eyes cutting through her webs of obfuscation and she wondered if, perhaps, someone had become suspicious when the old man had been found, if she had been seen on the bus near the supermarket, if someone had noticed her shoes. I'm tired, she said. Could I, please, go to sleep somewhere?

Seventeen

IN THE LATE afternoon the sunlight came thinly into the old house, one last rapier of light into the little sitting room that opened off the kitchen, thinner, paler beams almost like moonlight through the stairwell window. They awakened like children who have slept too long, neither knowing the time nor comprehending the day.

'I must find you some clothes to wear.' That was Louise, standing out on the upstairs landing with the faintly bewildered look of someone who imagines she has left herself behind somewhere. 'Is it Friday?' she said. 'Or Thursday? I seem to have lost track of the time. How long have we slept?' She no longer locked her bedroom door, hardly even closing it properly now. It swung gently sometimes in the breeze that came through the bedroom window or stood half open upon the view of Louise's furniture that had hardly changed since she was a small child. Her hoop-back oak bed, the dressing table that had, perhaps, once held her toys, then powder bowls and bracelets, and these days the handbag, worn at the corners, spilling its contents, the cheque book, the biro, a mirror into which she seldom looked now, the telephone bill, a notebook with doctor's appointments. Perhaps, in one of the lower drawers of the chest, the old passport might loiter, seriously out of date, with the visa stamps faded and nearly illegible. Hong Kong. Singapore. Frankfurt. London. Paris. Rome. Madrid. Home again. Not used thereafter.

Stephanie, still in the tender grip of the old kapok mattress, listened to the traffic outside. A modest but endless distant stream of cars heading towards the town, the shops, a supermarket at the bottom of the hill.

It must be Friday. The Friday shopping. All those people from up the road, some of whom she might actually once have known and others she might have recognised only by sight and other new people who had come to the town long after she left it and would not even know who she was or what she did or anything about her — it was all so long ago. They would all be rushing off to buy a Lotto ticket or a loaf of farmhouse cob bread or their own special fillet steak for Saturday night, fuel for their barbecues even though the weather was still chilly.

What are you doing out in the rain? they used to say to her sometimes and she would be made to go inside. What did you think you were doing out there? How long have you been there? Outside in this weather? What were you thinking of, to do something so silly? Nothing, she would say, I wasn't thinking of anything. Where I come from, the people take no notice of the rain. You must be mad to go outside in weather like this, just standing in it like that. Go and get dry. Go and put dry clothes on this instant. You must be mad, Stephanie. Well — and she would turn on them like a savage drowned dog — why don't you tell someone? That's what you've been trying to prove for years, isn't it? Why don't you say I'm mad? Go and change your clothes. The voices would be quieter then. Just go and change, Stephanie, and don't be silly. Are you trying to kill yourself, for heaven's sake? Yes. But that was in her own room, and later. Yes, indeed I am.

'Friday,' she said, 'I think it might be Friday, judging by the traffic. We've been asleep for hours,' she said, 'and I think it's definitely Friday,' she said. 'Clothes,' she said, 'clothes? I don't need any clothes. I haven't needed clothes for years, Louise. I don't go anywhere to wear nice clothes. I've got plenty of clothes for my needs. They give you clothes,' she said, and felt the shaft of her own brutality. 'You get given good, serviceable clothes to suit your needs and wants.' Talking now like some kind of guide book, she thought.

'I think you need a coat.' Louise was reaching up with her good arm now, feeling along the top of the panelling that lined the upstairs landing, the old wallpaper with its ancient fruit and hand-painted flowers just a rim along the top of those upper walls between the wainscotting and the ceiling. She held out a key. 'It's so long since I checked it was there

127

I suddenly thought it might have got lost somehow. Come with me. If I say you need a coat, you need a coat, and that's that.' They were all like that, she thought, the whole family. Finally, when they absolutely needed to, they would all turn and somehow could produce a flinty determination so inexorable that, like the susurrous waves upon a rocky shore, it would wear anything and anyone away. It would be useless to argue with Louise.

It seems to be useless to question you further, they said. Either you cannot or will not say anything more. I've told you all I know, she said, obdurate. I came here specifically to tell you. I brought the knife. I've told you what I did. I've told you a hundred times. I can't say anything more. Dogged and tenacious, she turned her face to the wall. I'm tired now. May I go to sleep? If you say there's an hour and thirty-five minutes unaccounted for, then there must be an hour and thirty-five minutes unaccounted for and that's that, but I can't tell you anything about it. I must have fainted, like I said, or gone into a dream. I don't remember. I can't help you. I can't recall what happened to that hour and thirty-five minutes. It seemed like no time at all to me, just a moment. I can't tell you what happened to that time. Please let me go to sleep now.

'Fine,' she said and threw back the blankets so suddenly that they made a slapping noise as they hit the end of the bed. Made dizzy by being upright, she stood on the rosy mat in her petticoat, nearly drunk with remembered sleep. 'Okay. A coat.' And then, when she had to grasp the end of the bed to stop herself staggering faintly, she said, 'Thank you. Thank you, Louise.'

This dress doesn't fit me, she had said once, perhaps after two or three years when she still had a recollection of vanity, of mirrors, of going out somewhere and feeling the swing of a well-tailored jacket from her shoulders. And I'm allergic to polyester, I'm sorry. Just wear it, they said. It's what you have to wear, so wear it. I was once a fashion editor. Too bad, you should have thought of that before you did it.

The old key faltered in the lock of the big bedroom across the landing, one of the rooms on the shady side of the house. Down the little corridor lay the tiny room she had slept in when she was a child and under its door came a thin and uninterrupted line of light. There must be nothing in there now to cast shadows, to stop the brightness from the high windows, she thought suddenly as Louise opened the old door and it swung open on nothing. Where once a grey and blue Persian carpet had lapped the floor with tides of fringes there were a few balls of dust on bare floorboards. There was no furniture.

'I don't come in here very often now.' Louise, though, walked across the bare room with great certainty, as if the emptiness were something that had become deeply familiar to her. 'There are still some things in the wardrobes, I think. I seem to remember a coat and a kimono and a few things, not that you'll be really needing a coat yet,' she said, 'because it's nearly summer. Perhaps we'll sort out a coat for you later, when there gets to be a bit of a nip in the air. Then we can come and get a coat for you, Stephanie.' Another narrower door swung open with a faint creak of hinges. 'I do hope the moths haven't got in.' She was rifling through the garments on the hangers now. An evening dress with a sequined bodice, a mauve tweed suit with a pair of parma violet suede gloves still neatly tucked in the tailored pocket, a man's cashmere greatcoat, something made of black chiffon, some hats formed entirely of silk flowers put away in tissue paper on an upper shelf, handbags packed in a carton on the floor, a pink brocade coat with buttons of sparkling glass. They were all great ones to dress up, she thought.

Aren't you coming? The voices used to seem impatient, echoing up the stairwell. There would always be someone using the door of the grandfather clock as a mirror, all the other looking glasses in the house taken up by cousins, aunts, friends. Does this hat look all right? Is my petticoat showing? Do these gloves match my dress? Do you think the brown? Or the blue? From the upstairs landing she used to watch them getting ready, sitting on the floor by the bathroom door to watch them through the banisters when she was a small child and, when she was older, loitering in the dim reaches of the dark upstairs hall. She's a plain little girl, isn't she? Some of the other aunts might say that. Not like my little girl. And they would thrust forward some plump child or another, an unfearful creature who had always proceeded under the impetus of her own perceived glory. My Elizabeth's always been such a beautiful child, haven't you Elizabeth, and Elizabeth would primp and nod. Show her some of your pretty steps from ballet, Elizabeth. Elizabeth goes to ballet. So there she would be, a prisoner of a prancing second cousin on the upstairs landing. Step-hop, step-hop, one, two, three, four, leap. Wasn't that pretty? Ask the little girl if she has dancing lessons, Elizabeth. She's too shy to answer. Well, never mind. We're all off now. If you sit on the floor like that, Stephanie, with your fingers spread out, someone might tread on your hand and you'll get your fingers pinched. Watch your dress, Elizabeth, when you're coming down the stairs. Don't run dear, you might pull some of the lace. That's right. That's a good girl. Wave goodbye.

When they had all gone to the races, the cars tooting in the drive, race books waving out the windows, see you later, good luck, meet you one o'clock sharp on the members' stand for lunch, she would go softly downstairs to the kitchen. We were too tired to go anyway, her mother would say. Just come here for a minute and let me fix that hair ribbon. I've saved you something nice for lunch. We'll have a nice chicken sandwich each, just you and me. We're going to have a good time here by ourselves, just the two of us. This afternoon we'll go for a walk. Run and put the kettle on and we'll have a cup of tea now they've gone. A long time later, perhaps as late as five o'clock, when they were starting to think about putting the dinner on, her mother would say carefully, You don't want to worry about that Elizabeth. She hasn't got very good bones, Stephanie. In the long run you're going to end up better-looking, I'd say. And we could have gone with them, you know. It wasn't that we couldn't have gone. We just didn't want to go. Auntie would have found me a hat and you could have worn your blue dress. But all that noise and shouting, I couldn't bear it. It's nice to have a quiet day. They — the pair of them — had loved silence, because their ordinary lives were so noisy. Shouting, slamming, the sound of blows, breaking china. Have you heard about poor — , and people would say her mother's name kindly, as if it might be an illness. She's left him again. She and the little girl have gone home to her family again. You could have come, you know, they would say when they all came racketing in the door in the early evening. We had a good day. The weather was perfect. We had a good win with Treasure O'Mine in the fourth race. You'd have been very welcome, you know. The track was hard and fast and everyone's in a good mood because *they didn't ruin their good shoes in the birdcage. What's for dinner? Oh good, my favourite.*

In the evening, when they had gone early to bed, she stood in her own front room trying the clothes on again, savouring the unaccustomed feel of the silks, the fur, the velour, the chiffon.

'It's rather an odd assortment,' Louise had said. 'Nothing really practical, but never mind.' She had always been a curiously effervescent girl, undeterred by things that cast other people down.

Louise has crashed up her car, that lovely new car her father bought her for her birthday. She recalled very well the talk echoing in her own childish ears. And there would be Louise, coming in the door for lunch from her office down town, from the bus stop over the road. Louise, whatever are you going to do about your nice new car, all crashed up like that? Lucky you weren't hurt. They say it's a write-off. There were always other cousins and aunts around the place eager to talk, to offer advice. And there would be Louise, with a cigarette held between red-tipped nails, and her long, slim legs posed delicately against the old fire-place while someone cleaned out the hearth. Don't you get any of those dirty wood ashes on my shoes, she'd say. They're shantung and they mark like crazy. And the car? She'd shrug. I suppose I'll just go and get another one. I think I'll get a red one next time, it might be luckier. People might see me coming. Hello, Stephanie, are you here again with Mummy? Be a good girl and pass me that telephone book, will you? I've just got to give someone a tinkle. If you look in my bag there might be a liquorice allsort down the bottom that hasn't gone too fuzzy.

'Now, try this coat on. I know it's nearly summer and far too hot to wear it, but I think it'd look lovely on.' And there she had been, captured by that blurred and accidental looking glass made by the window, in the red coat, its soft velour almost like velvet and the dyed fox trim around the wrists making her hands look very long and very pale. 'Wonderful. Keep that. Put that aside for the winter.' Louise was delving in the wardrobe again. 'Somewhere in here,' she was saying, the voice muffled by clothing, 'there's a black georgette dress that might be just the thing for you.' There was silence for a moment, then an exclamation of satisfaction. 'Oh, try this on in the meantime.' An arm thrust forth a loose floppy blouse.

'I've never worn mauve.'

'It isn't mauve. It's Parma violet. Try it on. I think it might suit you.'

Humour her as much as possible, they had said as she left in the car, just before the hand went slap-slap on the roof and someone said, Off you go then — cheerio. No one knows what the prognosis really will be. Just let her do anything within reason that makes her happy. There are often remissions if a person becomes happy and tranquil, if they are unfearful. Just do the best you can to keep her on a very even keel and she can do anything she wants to do within reason.

'Are you quite sure —' She stopped there. It might be a mistake to say, 'Are you quite sure you feel all right?' Best to leave Louise searching the old wardrobe, laughing from within silken draperies. 'Are you quite sure you're warm enough?' she said.

'Try this.' Louise had found the black dress, had not heard the question. 'Take that coat off and put this on. Oh yes,' she said when the thin old silk had slipped easily over Stephanie's head, and her arms were thrust into those long, graceful sleeves, 'Oh yes, you must have that. Come into my bedroom and look at yourself in a proper mirror, not just that silly old window.' And there she had been, the creature she once recalled, a person she had thought was completely gone, her own self back again. Thinner. Paler. Older. But back again.

'You'll be wondering why that bedroom is empty, why so many of the rooms are empty.' Louise stood beside her, addressing her reflection in the mirror as if they were hairdressers, able only to converse with or confide in images in a looking glass. 'There was far too much stuff here, anyway,' said Louise, 'and I'd always meant to sell some, to sort it out. You know how you sort things out sometimes?'

'Yes.' And that was another lie, another piece of well-intentioned mendacity because she had not sorted anything out at the end. Other people had done that. Her house. Her furniture. Her clothes. Her jewellery.

'And you needed things, Stephanie. Lawyers, and things like that. You needed things. It all cost a lot. It had to be paid for.' The reflections in the mirror wavered a little. A small breeze from the window was ruffling the glass, blurring the images. One figure/two figures. Both of them nearly the same height, the same colour hair, the same high cheek bones, faces different but oddly the same, the same nose, the same shuttered look. 'I don't even think about what I sold. I didn't need it, anyway, and I was glad to be rid of it all. There was far too much for me to look after all by myself, there was really.'

Hello, Stephanie, are you and Mummy back again? There would be Louise, fresh from the office, again idly standing against the dining room fireplace and tapping one immaculately shod toe in a blue, slightly lustrous, pearly shoe. We'd better pop you upstairs, hadn't we, and see if we can find you a jersey or something. It's a bit cold, dear, to be going around with bare arms like that. We left in a bit of a hurry. That would be her mother, standing in the kitchen door, with an apron on. I'm just making some soup. Might as well make myself useful. Stephanie, be a good girl and don't get in the way. Louise is a great big grown-up girl now and she doesn't want to be bothered with a little girl hanging around. Just come back here in the kitchen. But they had gone by then, her mother's voice fading away down the stairs. Race you to the top of the stairs, and Louise had leapt along in her high-heeled shoes while Louise's father said, You'll both break your necks one of these days, running up the stairs like that, you two. And how do you expect me to be able to read the paper with a noise like that going on, like a herd of elephants?

'It doesn't really matter, Stephanie, not even slightly. I mean, I never used these rooms anyway. It's years since anyone slept in them, or stayed here. There's no one left, except you and me, Stephanie, so who cares if the bedroom suites in those other two rooms have gone. And the carpets — well, they were worn out anyway.'

Where's my ring? I've lost my good ring. It was race day again, and one of the relatives, perhaps a well-upholstered distant great-aunt or a second cousin, was on all fours on the carpet. I'll ladder my nylons. I'll have to go to the races with a ladder in my nylons if I crawl around like this. Come and help me find my ring, Stephanie. In you go. That would be her mother, giving her a little push. In you go, Stephanie. See if you

133

can find the pretty ring. Make yourself useful. So there they had been, a small girl in a smocked dress that tied behind her waist with two ribbons and someone in a coat with a beaver collar, large pearl earrings and surrounded by the scent of l'Air du Temps, powder spilling from a newly opened box on the dressing table and a silken scarf thrown over the edge of the mirror. Hurry up, May, we'll never get there before the first race. A man in a grey pin-striped suit and a soft felt hat, lighting a cigarette, waiting out on the landing. You women and your outfits. If I had a penny for every time you've kept everyone waiting, I'd have a fortune. I can't help it, Fred. The light in this bedroom's just terrible. I've dropped my ring on the carpet and I'm not going without it. It's my Brazilian yellow diamond and it's my lucky ring. God help us, don't let anyone tread on it. Oh good, she's found it. In the deep pile of the Persian rug the old ring had loitered, caught in the woven traceries of flowers and garlands, and for an instant the light from the high casements caught the facets on the stone so the ring rested on her own finger like a drop of water, like a huge tear from the eye of the window.

'I've never asked you many questions,' she had said to him once, towards the end. 'Perhaps I have a horror of questions, I don't know. When I was a child I used to hate questions. People used to ask me questions about my father if they didn't dare ask anyone else. I always thought it was an obscure form of bullying. So I don't like questions. I'm not a questioner. I've never asked you many questions and often, now, I wish I had.'

'Well, fire away,' he said, but she thought he took on an uneasy look, a trifle flushed with nonchalance, and genuine nonchalance, she thought, should not make a man flush. 'Ask me anything you like.'

'For instance' — and she stabbed the butter lightly before spreading it on a scrap of French bread — 'why, when I first met you and you told me about yourself, did your story end when you left your wife and went and lived in a flat somewhere? Why was that the end of the story when it wasn't the end at all?'

'How do you mean?' He had stopped eating, though, she noticed that. 'I did go and live in a flat when I left my wife.'

'Indeed you did. But there was more to it, wasn't there? You left your wife and you went and lived in a flat. Then you met someone else and got married again and went and lived in a large house somewhere else entirely.'

'Oh that,' he said. 'Well, perhaps we got interrupted at that point. Perhaps I just forgot to tell you the rest and you never asked.'

'I'd like to go out with you sometimes.' She had been persistent that day, relentless in her own way. Unusual. Uncharacteristic. 'Some places I go, well, the people say I could take someone with me if I liked. You know — they say I could take a partner if I liked.'

'Where?' His voice was quite sharp.

'Oh just people's places, people I know. If I go out to dinner sometimes they say, 'Bring a friend if you'd like, Stephanie, bring someone with you, bring a partner if you'd like.' I'd like to take someone with me, I'd like to take you so I'm not always by myself, so I'm not always the only one there by myself. I always make the numbers wrong. I'm always an odd number. I wish I could take you. I wish I had someone to take.' And much later she said, 'If I had known at the beginning what I do now — oh never mind, never mind.'

Your mother was once a very pretty girl. That was Louise's father, holding out a box of chocolates. From his large armchair by the fireplace he watched the activities of the household, novel in one hand, box of sweets in the other. Out in the entrance hall her mother was vacuuming the carpet with wide, rhythmic, sweeping movements, her arms thickened by work and age. If you take that one in the middle of the first row, Stephanie, I think you'll find it's got a soft centre, that one with the pink paper. Yes, that one. Did May and Fred thank you for finding her ring? Well, if they didn't, they should have. I think I might be able to find a silver penny for a good girl. And while she squashed the chocolate against the roof of her mouth he fished in his pockets for a florin or a half a crown. If we were all as clever at the beginning as we are at the end the world might be a different place, Stephanie. He was still watching her mother as she worked. I remember the first time your mother brought your father here for us to meet. She was a very beautiful girl then. Anyway, he said, never mind, never mind. Whatever would we do without you to find jewellery for the ladies when they lost it? Every house should have one — a good little girl to find things. As I said, if we were all as wise at the beginning as we are at the end.

The silence had lengthened and the lunch table looked, she thought, tawdry, the flowers past their best, the food mediocre, the avocado browning at the edges in a salad that had seemed tasteless.

'Whatever would I do without you,' he said, 'to get me a nice little lunch sometimes?' And he had looked at her in a cheerful kind of way, as if he might be jollying her along somehow, gilding it all with jocularity.

'Does your wife ever mislay her jewellery?'

He was in the middle of taking a sip of wine and she watched as his hand jumped slightly, the liquid within the glass spilling.

'What a peculiar thing to say, Stephanie.'

'I don't think it's peculiar at all. If she lost her jewellery you could call me in to find it. You could put it on my list of tasks, like getting lunch sometimes, and not asking questions, like not going places with anyone and always being just at home.'

'I don't know what's got into you today. You're never usually like this.'

'I know,' she said and stood up, walked over to the little chiffonier to get a spoon out of the drawer, looked at her own pale face in the old mottled mirror.

'Do you know' — he had picked up a little jar of apple chutney — 'that this has reached its use-by date? This chutney I've just put on my beef has reached its use by date? Stephanie?'

'Has it?' And that was when she looked past the spoons, right to the back of the drawer where the old carving knife was kept.

'Stephanie,' he said, 'what are you doing? What do you think you're do —'

Eighteen

IN THE MORNING the telephone rang, as it usually did, just after they both went downstairs, the stairwell still slightly steamy from Louise's bath and scented faintly by the bath cubes they had dissolved in the warm water. The days, at first so separate, each one a marker in the dispersal of time, had somehow grown blurred at the edges, one week becoming another gently and slowly. The hours, too, became indecipherable till they looked at the old clock in the hall.

'Ten o'clock.' That would be one of them. 'Not eleven o'clock at all. We've got one more hour that we didn't know we had,' and, grinning like children on holiday, they would wait for the kettle to boil. 'Morning tea, then, not a very early lunch after all. Tomato sandwich? Okay then.' They would, by then, have gone through the questioning routine. Yes, they were fine. No, there was no sign of the patient wanting to go away. There was nothing to report. All was well. Thank you. Goodbye.

'We'll just have to wait and see.' That was the surgeon the previous week, busy with the scissors while Louise held her arm up like a wing, Stephanie a sentinel by the examining couch.

'This is my cousin,' Louise had said when they went into the surgery. 'She's the one I've told you about, the one who came to look after me.'

That the surgeon looked at her in an assessing way, Stephanie thought, could have been imagination. Perhaps he had wondered if she cooked meals that were nourishing enough, had been sufficiently kind about making the bed, changing the linen. Perhaps he thought she may need surgery herself. Possibly there might be an incipient benign cyst forming on her left temple, undiscernible except to a trained eye, a tendency to favour the left leg, thus resulting in too much wear on that knee joint (more surgery). Perhaps anything. Or nothing.

But Louise, sitting very still like an animal trapped, had said, 'We are rather alike to look at,' to perhaps deflect his possible suspicion that he had seen Stephanie before, might have remembered a picture in a newspaper, a hint of the trial. She noted also that she did not plainly state her own name then but remained, standing silently, a kind of unspecified relative who could have been called anything and could have come from anywhere. So that was the visit to the surgeon dealt with and they went quietly home after that, the next appointment card carefully placed in Louise's handbag like a pressed leaf from a lost season.

'Early days yet,' he had said but smiled as he spoke so on the way home they stopped and bought an ice cream each, again as if they were children and had everything to look forward to.

'Last one to finish her ice cream lives to ninety-two,' said Stephanie. 'There you are, Louise, you've won.'

'You ate yours quickly, on purpose.'

'No, I didn't. Where I come from everyone eats quickly and has short hair.' They were, she thought, becoming more frank.

The ringing of the telephone in the early morning was the only call that was always answered, though sometimes the telephone pealed at other times of the day.

'You answer it,' Louise would say, so Stephanie used to listen to her own bland well-meaning falsehoods to strangers on the other end of the line. Louise had just slipped out for a moment over to the shops. She was absolutely fine and was doing well. She would ask Louise to ring back in a minute, as soon as she returned. In the evenings they threw the pieces of paper that held the scribbled telephone numbers into the fire. But the morning call was marked on their minds, Louise mostly rising from the breakfast table to deal with it and her replies always the same. Yes, they were quite all right. No, her cousin Stephanie showed no sign of leaving or wanting to leave. Everything was excellent. Yes, the meals were very good and she was feeling better. Yes, Mrs Beaumont — Stephanie — seemed quiet and was sleeping better than she had done. Her bedroom light went off earlier at night, the nightmares were less frequent, they were both happy in the house just doing the chores. Nightmares? Everyone has nightmares sometimes. It was just that her cousin, Mrs

Beaumont, sometimes seemed to have bad dreams and cried out in her sleep, but she seemed to be getting better, seemed to be more tranquil. Yes, thank you — everything's fine. Goodbye.

But this morning the conversation took longer, the voice became raised. 'I want her to stay. We aren't doing any harm. We're just quietly here in the old house. There's very little left. Most of the rooms are empty now. I've sold nearly everything. What more do you want? You've taken everything — just let us live quietly here by ourselves. I want her to stay. I don't want her to go back at the end of the month. I want her to stay. She's to stay here with me. I want her to stay here with me.' The vehemence of it was a surprise, like the wife at the trial, firmly planted on thick legs, the voice raised, the colour high.

My husband and I were devoted. I don't believe what she says. She must be mad. She must be disturbed to say such a thing. Certainly he was sometimes absent from the house on business but that isn't unusual. We loved each other. He said he loved me. He always said he loved me. He was the soul of kindness to me, the soul of courtesy. Never at any time were we on ill terms. He always said he loved me. He told me every day that he loved me. I don't believe he saw her regularly, had seen her regularly for years. She's a liar. What she says is lies. I think he had to call on her that day somehow as a matter of business and she inexplicably killed him because she's mad. How should I know what business? I don't know what business they might have had to discuss. My husband loved me. We were perfectly happy. Everyone said so. Everyone knew how happy we were, how well-suited we were. He did everything for me, just everything. No one ever had a better husband. I don't believe he had someone else all those years. I don't believe it. What she says is lies from beginning to end. My health? My own health? No, there's nothing the matter with me at all. I don't know what you're talking about. I have no long-term illness, no hereditary condition. I'm a perfectly healthy, normal woman. We led a perfectly healthy, normal life. My husband loved me. If she says that my husband turned to her for solace because I'm an invalid she's a liar.

'I've told them that you're staying, that I want you to stay.' Louise was coming back into the kitchen now, closing the door behind her with a quick, sharp movement like a person cutting something off, carving something unpleasant off a piece of meat that was otherwise good. 'And I've had an idea,' she said. 'I've been thinking about it ever since you arrived. What we're going to do next time you take me out in the car is look around in second-hand shops for a dolls' pram.'

'A dolls' pram?' The teacup placed quickly and carelessly on the saucer made a small noise like a ring falling on a table.

Will you please take your jewellery off? Please place all your valuables on this table. But can't I keep my wedding ring on? No, everything must be taken off. But I've never taken it off since it was put on. It might not come off. If it won't come off I'll call someone to cut it off. And they had done that, the little ring falling on to the tabletop. It wasn't my husband I killed, she said. It was another man, later. If my husband had not died none of this would have happened. If wishes were horses, beggars would ride.

'Yes, a dolls' pram.' Louise was pouring more tea now as if she might be the nurse and Stephanie in need of care. 'You've mentioned that old dolls' pram several times. Well, we'll go and get a dolls' pram from somewhere. There must be an old dolls' pram for sale somewhere, mustn't there? We'll find one and we'll buy it. And then,' she said, 'we'll look around for a couple of old china dolls to put in it and we'll get it all set up on the landing, just like you remember.'

Outside the kitchen windows there was a sudden flurry in the garden and the cat sprang on to the wall, beginning to wash its face, preening its fur in the sun.

'There's that cat again.' Stephanie looped her index finger through the handle of her teacup, concentrated on keeping the hand very still, held her breath. In some ways, she thought, their clearly understood reticence would make their ends easier.

She said she'd just close her eyes for a minute while I went and made her a cup of tea. She said she had a fancy to have a cup of tea. When I brought it back I thought she'd gone to sleep but I bent over her to awaken her and I saw that she'd gone. And which one of them would it be, she thought — the first to die? My cousin Stephanie came to look after me once when I was ill and then she stayed on. One day she just died very quietly in her sleep. It was her heart, they said. Her heart had somehow been affected by her hard life. She'd led a hard life, really, Stephanie, my cousin. Or would it be the other way round? She made a wonderful recovery but the illness left its mark. I'd put the kettle on to make her afternoon tea and I found her when I took her tray in. Her face was very peaceful. Like twins, in tandem, cousins. The same colouring. The same thoughts. The same ideas. Do you see that big house over there? For a long time just one lady lived in it, then her sister or cousin or someone who looked very like her came and lived there with her. Would people say things like that? Talking idly? We used to see them about a lot together and they always seemed very happy and very quiet and nice. Then one died and the other one died not long after and then a family bought the place and lives there now. Or it's been turned into offices — it was such a big place. Into doctors' consulting rooms. Anything. We've always remembered the two ladies who lived there, though. We called them 'The Sisters'. Even though they might not have been sisters. The butcher knew them. He'd be able to tell you, if you asked. They always seemed happy. They had a cat and someone once told me they collected old dolls, that they'd spend hours making clothes for the dolls out of old lace. It was what you might call their hobby.

'You did say that you'd like the cat to stay, didn't you?' Stephanie went to the refrigerator. 'I think I'll give it a little bit of that cold meat we've got left over. It might like some breakfast, don't you think?' She chose an old saucer from the cupboard, went to the door with the squares of meat placed on the dish like stamps on a welcoming letter. *This is a lonely place. Do, please, come to stay for as long as you like. Our lives are very quiet but you'd be most welcome.* 'There you are,' she said to the cat and watched it eat. 'There you are,' she said to Louise. 'You've got a cat. It doesn't really matter if it lives somewhere else. Cats are very duplicitous. I'm sure it can pretend it lives here for some of the day before it goes home to where it really lives.'

So there it was. A cat. A dolls' pram. Dolls.

'It might be a nice day today.' Louise was watching the cat eat the meat. 'What name do you think?'

'Gwendolyn or Humphrey. Depending.' It was best to prevaricate swiftly and blatantly, to turn the doubts into vigorous certainties, she thought. 'But not Bonzo. I couldn't stand a cat, an animal, called Bonzo, please. Yes, I think it will. Be a fine day, I mean. Perhaps that second-hand shop we've often driven past down the road, perhaps they might have one?'

'We could ask anyway.' Louise sipped her tea. 'Marvellous,' she said. 'Exactly how I like it. The man might be able to tell us where to get one, even if he didn't have one in stock himself.' Their athletic loops of conversation had taken them back to the dolls' pram. 'Oh by the way,' she said, 'they told me this morning' — and she nodded towards the hall where the telephone had always sat on its own wooden shelf — 'that they've given permission for someone to come and see you.'

'See me?'

'Yes, someone's coming to see you tomorrow. Someone who used to know you and who might be driving through town tomorrow. He'll drop in tomorrow to say hello, if he's got time.' She took a bite of the toast. 'Too sweet,' she said. 'Next time we make marmalade we'll take one orange out of the recipe and put in another lemon instead.'

'Marmalade?' Her own toast remained on the plate unbuttered, untouched.

'You'd better eat your breakfast.' Louise was pouring another cup of tea. 'Or you won't have enough strength to see your visitor. Yes, marmalade. I've told them I want you to stay so, presumably, you'll be here next year for the marmalade season, when the grapefruit tree and the orange tree have their fruit. So you'll be here then and we must remember to put more lemons in the recipe, so it's more tart. And, talking about tarts, there's some short pastry in the freezer, I think, and plenty of raspberry jam, so after breakfast we'll make some jam tarts.' Louise seemed suddenly to possess great energy, secrets, ideas.

'Jam tarts?'

'Yes, jam tarts. Pass me your cup. I suppose you want another cup of tea? Yes, jam tarts — for your visitor. He'll need something for his afternoon tea. So when we've been to the second-hand shop to ask about the dolls' pram we might just nip around the corner and get some fresh bread for sandwiches. We could have a nice little tray of sandwiches for him as well. We could get out the garden chairs and set them out in the old dining room. If we pulled the blinds up and let the sun in it might look quite homely, do you think?'

'You've left me behind,' she said. 'I don't know who you mean. No one would come to see me. I've never had anyone visiting me, not for years. You were the only one who even wrote to me. I wish you wouldn't joke about it. I haven't got anyone to come and see me.'

The cat had spread itself out in a sunny patch inside the kitchen door and lay there, watching them carefully through narrow golden eyes.

'What about your car? Who was it who looked after your car and kept it up on blocks?' Louise was enticing, smiling, like a presenter of a game show. 'Well, that's the one who's coming to see you. A Russell Something.' None of them were good at remembering names. 'Just lean down, will you, and open the door of the freezer — that's right. If you pull out that flat parcel just inside the door, that's the one, that's short pastry. For the tarts, Stephanie, for the jam tarts. And what a shame,' she said, 'that I didn't keep the tea wagon. I sold it years ago. Never mind, we've got trays.'

In that peculiar transference of thought they all possessed, she could understand immediately that Louise saw them having afternoon tea in the old dining room, the sun slanting through the windows and the tea wagon rattling along on the bare floorboards just as it had done years ago but there was carpet then and the wagon's passage was smoother. *If you're a very good little girl, Stephanie, you can have a piece of cream sponge but only if you sit down very carefully on this chair and let me tie this dinner napkin round your neck.* An endless stream of afternoon teas had been served in the house and this would be another one, a late, lost afternoon tea when they had both thought all they would ever do, for the rest of their lives, was put a teabag in a saucerless cup of boiling water and stand moodily drinking a brown liquid of no recognisable taste while they stared out the kitchen window at the rhubarb.

'I wonder if he takes milk and sugar? I wonder if I can find a sugar bowl and a milk jug that match. Is he a nice man? Would he rather have a beer?'

'No, he'd rather have afternoon tea. I'm sure he'd rather have a jam tart and a cup of tea.' *Thank you, Russell, cheerio. See ya, Stephanie. How many years ago had that been?*

'I think I'll ask him about my front left tyre. It might have a slow puncture.' Louise, suddenly, seemed assured and confident as a caterer. 'I could take him out to the shed to have a look at it while the kettle's boiling. They said he knew all about cars.'

In the secret depths of the night, when the faint aroma of cooked jam tarts had wafted up the stairs to scent their bedrooms, Stephanie lay, only half awake, in the grip of the tender mattress. Perfectly easily, with no effort, she remembered the words emblazoned on the façade of Russell's old garage, the blue pebbledash as bright as the sky and Russell standing there saying, 'I saw you coming down the street so I came out to say hello.' SEASPRAY LAUNDRY.

The shadows fall with gentle clarity at twilight on the lonely margins of the sea and, sometimes, people might come laughing down the dunes with a picnic basket, a parcel of jam tarts tied within a dinner napkin. I had almost forgotten what you looked like, it was so long ago, but I remember now. You haven't changed at all. Except for my hair, she said. It's shorter now. Give it a month or two — it'll be okay. How funny you should say that, she said. That's exactly what my cousin says.

Nineteen

'SHE MAY REMEMBER later.' That was one of the men sitting at the big table, one of the men with a notebook and a folder full of sheets of paper.

'I might,' she said. 'I could very well remember later. An hour and thirty-five minutes is quite a long time. Perhaps,' she said, 'I might have kind of fainted standing up, like horses go to sleep. Horses sleep standing up. Or I think they sleep standing up. I think I read somewhere that horses sleep standing up. I'm not becoming repetitive, am I? Am I repeating myself? I'm tired. I'm over-tired.' She waited. 'Do you think I could possibly have kind of become unconscious with, say, fear or horror or something like that but stayed standing up and all that time went by?' They turned and conferred with each other then, faces closer together, voices even lower. They had begun to be slightly careless, faint dismissal in their eyes, discussing her so she could hear clearly what they said, so now they became more discreet, attentive to the timbre of their own voices, aware of the carrying quality of their words. 'She doesn't look the type,' one of them had said earlier, 'not the type — well,' he said, 'you know what I mean.'

'I do agree with you.' Her voice, from the other side of the table, had contained a quality of reticence she would not have thought possible. Already, in her ears, the years were echoing, the long, glad run up the thin hall of her cottage — 'Oh, you've come, you've come after all.' So she would look back to the little kitchen where there might be a large country pie cooking wastefully because she had thought he could not visit that day. There might have been one of those elusive calls in the early morning, the voice muffled, sounds of crowds in the background. Perhaps a telephone at the supermarket.

'I can't come today after all. She's sick. She's performing again. She's having hysterics. She's run out of her pills. I can't leave her like this.' But the pastry would be already mixed by then, the steak and kidney filling simmering on the stove, so she would have made the pie later with no sense of gladness, just because the ingredients were there and she could not afford to waste them.

'She got her pills,' he would say as he stepped through the front door. 'The doctor got a delivery boy to bring them. She seemed calmer. She went to see her sister. I've slipped away. Didn't have time to ring again, sorry.' And what, a moment before, had been silence and stillness would become laughter. The pie in the oven, as if sensing the excitement, would make its pastry rise perfectly, the whole tableau like a painting in a book of still lifes when she placed the food on the old wooden table among the silver and the blue plates and said, 'There you are then, spoilt brat.' A work of art. Naive Still Life of Unknown Woman with Pie and Old China, Figure of Man Turning Away in Background, Artist Unknown, Uncatalogued, Provenance Uncertain.

Defendant seemed to talk wildly. She mentioned horses. She mentioned that she thought she was a horse and that she slept standing up. At no time did she give any reasonable explanation of what happened during the time lapse, said the sergeant. I could not sort out the meaning of what she said. When asked what she had done during the unexplained one hour and thirty-five minutes defendant said she had turned into a horse and had gone to sleep.

I did not say that. I did not. I said nothing of the sort. That was me, standing up. That was me, raising my voice. I said nothing of the sort, I said. I never said I was a horse. What a ridiculous thing to say. I have never in my life claimed to be a horse. What I actually said was — But I was cut off there, and rightfully so because it was not my turn to speak. Will you please sit down? Will you remain silent, please, or you will be in contempt of court.

Did anyone see this woman? There is my picture on a million, on two million, television screens during *Crimewatch*. I look thin and old, my hair too flat against my head. I am flashed on the screen full-face and side-on, the number at the base of the picture a disturbing little ratchet of figures like a barbed wire fence. Please telephone our 0800 number if you think you saw this woman between the hours of this and that on such-and-such a day. No one rang in. But people saw me. There was the bus driver to whom I made a vague explanation about my stained shoes. When I paid my fare I noticed a dark ring of blood under my fingernails that other people may also have seen. A woman with dirty, blood-marked hands. 'Nice day,' said the person I sat next to. 'Super,' I said, and tucked my feet under the seat. I had gone to the corner and caught the bus home straightaway because it came into my mind that the next person I might like to kill would be my old headmistress. You are not destined for success. I still recall her thin, dry voice, filled with such certainty. Perhaps she was right. So I would have liked to kill my father, and in an odd way I did. I certainly made him die. His death was precipitated by me. I stood there thinking how easy it would be to become a mass murderer. Years later someone once said to me, 'Do you see that woman over there? She killed two people. Can you imagine it? Can you imagine anyone, a woman, killing two people?' 'Yes,' I said. 'Easy-peasy.' And I went on making bags on a commercial sewing machine, thundering along the side seams. We were taught to sew. I said over the noise, 'It's easy enough done. Killing two people's easy. Once you've killed one, it's only one more.' I went on sewing. After that the bell rang and we had our lunch. Two Marmite sandwiches and an apple. 'Did you really mean what you said earlier? About it being easy to kill two people?' The woman came up to me again before we filed out to our rooms. 'Yes,' I said, 'I meant every word of it.' 'Well,' she said, 'how many did you kill then?' 'One,' I said. 'You don't know what you're talking about, do you,' she said. 'How would you know anything about it.'

Have you ever had any urge to kill anyone else? That was one of the notebook men, I forget when. Have I ever had any urge to kill anyone else? Why would I want to do that, I said. It was not a lie. So you've never had any other urge to kill anyone? Who, I said, and why? Who would I kill, and why — I ask you? I sounded innocent. May I go back to my sewing now? May I go back to the garden? May I go to my room now, please, I don't feel well.

Perhaps it was more cruel of me to let my father die voluntarily, killed by his own sudden terror, having choked slowly on his own poisoned system for years. Perhaps flies were attracted to him even before he stiffened. Flies can gather in a minute. Who could say how many there might be in an hour.

What are you thinking about at this exact moment? The man with the notebook again. Um, I said, flies. Flies? Yes, it's summer. There seem to be a lot of flies around. And at the same time, kind of in tandem somehow in my own mind, I was thinking about jewellery. Why were you thinking about jewellery? Once, I said, a long time ago, I had really nice jewellery. I had a little ruby brooch shaped like a spider — not a fly — with diamond chips for eyes, and I had a very pretty sapphire necklace like a bunch of grapes. Not real, surely? Yes, it was all real. Most of the stones were quite large and a good colour. My husband bought it all for me once, a long time ago, when things were different, before I was like I am now. It was a long, long time ago. I thought everything would be nice forever then. See the lightning, I said, but you think the thunderstorm will never be overhead, it happens only to other people. I'm not sure I follow your drift, he said, it seems to be a fine day to me but I could be wrong in that. You can go to your room if you want to. It's been a long day. What medication are they giving you these days?

Twenty

IT IS A lie that the lonely margins of the sea
are, in fact, lonely and that all you find there is rubbish tossed up by the
ocean. The lonely margins of the sea are truly not untenanted. Believe
this. If you see an empty shore it is empty only for a moment, for an hour
or two between visitors. It might be only forty minutes before another
fisherman arrives after the last one left at the turn of the tide.

The shore is a beautiful, kind, tenanted place and when people are not
present there are always the sea birds conducting their elaborate rituals
of flight and feeding, dancing on the wet sand with fragile feet to leave
marks like those of an arcane language. *You are welcome here. This is a
beautiful place. The rocks, the foam, the shore are your friends. It is not a
lonely place and you are not lonely. You are alone, that is all, not lonely.*

Every day this week they have come to this shore, the man with two
women, the women oddly alike in colouring, though one is older than
the other and walks carefully. One arm is held across her chest as if
guarding it. The other woman carries a picnic basket in which she has a
cake tin, cups and saucers, a thermos flask. It is not the sort of picnic that
you see much these days. Mostly people bring takeaways on plastic
plates, bags of fried chicken and chips, fruit juice in cardboard containers. But these people have a picnic like people used to have. Their cater-
ing is old-fashioned. They spread out a rug behind a rock, they all sit
down carefully, the younger woman lifting aside the covering of the basket.

'Jam tarts,' said the man the second day they were there. 'It must be
a good while since I had a jam tart two days running.'

'Just be careful of the pastry.' That was the younger woman, the silent one who had not spoken till now. 'I made it myself and home-made pastry's inclined to crumble. I was going to use the bought, but home-made's nicer.' She has an air of silence and stillness seen only in animals that are caged at the zoo, in creatures that have been shut away. 'What do you think you might like for tomorrow?' she says. 'For when we come down here tomorrow? You can't have the same thing to eat every day, you know. You had jam tarts yesterday, only that was bought pastry with raspberry jam. Today it's home-made, with strawberry. But there's got to be variety. And we're running out of jam.'

'That's okay,' said the man. 'We can stop at the supermarket on the way home and get some more and after that I'll drop in to a garage somewhere and pick up a new set of spark plugs — I think she's missing a beat along the line somewhere even though I've given her a bit of a tune-up.' He nodded towards the car, which they had left parked at the top of the sandhills. 'And I think you might be right about that slow puncture, but I'll check that tomorrow, or the day after. There's plenty of time,' and he held out his cup. 'Thanks,' he said. 'Milk and no sugar.'

'Perhaps,' she said, 'if they haven't got raspberry we could try the cherry,' and she began to believe, in her own peculiar way, that he understood the loops and whorls of the way she spoke — the way their whole family conversed — and would know she was talking about jam. Ten out of ten.

The margins of the sea are not lonely. Even when people go home, the mark of their feet still lies in the sand like a pattern for dancing till the tide comes in. Meanwhile the seabirds wheel and call to each other endlessly, perhaps in imitation of what they have heard. There are some who say that mynahs can imitate laughter and the sound of a telephone ringing. Mynahs, and seabirds.